Franny tapped her pen impatiently on her desk and pulled at her lip. What was she to do?

Then it came to her. Just because nothing had happened in her life didn't mean she couldn't *make* something happen. She wrote, "I will make something happen." Immediately another thought came to her. Was it possible that things *were* happening which she had not noticed? Things that were just as exciting as anything she had read about? This idea changed everything. "I will make it my business to unearth the events that must be quietly erupting in my family," she wrote. "I will unearth them, explode them, and record them. I will go at least two steps further than any girl I've read about lately."

SHEILA GREENWALD, a native New Yorker, has written a number of other books for young readers including *All the Way to Wit's End*, which is available in a Yearling edition.

It All Began
with
JANE EYRE

Sheila Greenwald

For David, Amy, Laura,
and Nancy Goldin

LAUREL-LEAF BOOKS bring together under a single imprint outstanding works of fiction and nonfiction particularly suitable for young adult readers, both in and out of the classroom. Charles F. Reasoner, Professor Emeritus of Children's Literature and Reading, New York University, is consultant to this series.

Published by
Dell Publishing Co., Inc.
1 Dag Hammarskjold Plaza
New York, New York 10017

Laurel-Leaf Library ® TM 766734, Dell Publishing Co., Inc.

ISBN: 0-440-94136-9

RL: 5.5

Reprinted by arrangement with
Little, Brown and Company, Inc.

Printed in the United States of America

October   1981

10 9 8 7 6 5 4

1

"My mother thinks it all began with *Jane Eyre*," Franny Dillman wrote in her journal. She paused to remember those days—only weeks before—when she had been reading *Jane Eyre*. She'd read the book by flashlight at the back of her closet.

She recalled the fateful afternoon, when, as was her habit, she had settled down with a bag of potato chips, a box of gingersnaps, a bottle of celery tonic, and her dog-eared paperback, to the happiest moments of her day. She sat in a clearing between two stacks of shoes. The top of her head was brushed by the bottoms of three plastic wardrobe bags and a selection of skirts. Her nostrils breathed in the pleasant aroma of camphor. With the greasy fingers of one hand she would turn pages and select chips and cookies, while in the other hand she held

the flashlight by which she read. In the closet, Jane
Eyre's woes were Franny's torments; Jane's passions, her passions; Jane's suffering, her very òwn
despair. Her eyes moved from left to right, her jaw
from north to south as she rhythmically chomped
and reread, with fast-beating pulse and for the
twentieth time, Mr. Rochester's first avowal of love
for Jane Eyre. Ahhhhh. *Chomp, chomp, chomp.*

"My bride is here," he said, again drawing
me to him, "because my equal is here, and my
likeness. Jane, will you marry me?"
Still I did not answer, and still I writhed
myself from his grasp: for I was still incredu-
lous.

"Why on earth are you reading in the closet?"
Mrs. Dillman's voice boomed on the other side of
the closet door. "We bought you that reading lamp
with the high-intensity bulb. You have a desk and
a chair and a bed. For heaven's sake, Franny, *Jane
Eyre* is a classic. Do come out of the closet."
"I like it in here," Franny growled.
"But Franny, do you think it's good for you?"
Her mother's voice throbbed with concern. She
opened the door a crack so that a shaft of daylight
fell on Franny's sneakered feet. They both blinked.
"Look, darling," Mrs. Dillman went on after a
pause, "perhaps you read too much."
"What do you mean?" Franny turned off her

flashlight and glanced up at her mother suspiciously.

"You know." Mrs. Dillman fidgeted.

"You mean, Mr. Crawford again."

"Yes, as a matter of fact." Mrs. Dillman stood her ground. "All that would never have happened if not for *Jane Eyre*."

"That's what I thought you meant," Franny said hotly. "If Mary Beth Higgens hadn't blabbed to her mother nothing would have happened."

"But sweetheart, *you* were the one who told all your friends that Mrs. Crawford was crazy like Mrs. Rochester in *Jane Eyre*, and that she had to be watched by someone just like Grace Poole, and that Mr. Crawford was suffering exactly as Mr. Rochester had suffered."

By now Franny's mood was hopelessly shattered. She put her book down and got out of the closet. "I only told Rosy Shuloff," she said regretfully. "Rosy told Mary Beth. Mary Beth told her mother. Mary Beth's mother told Mrs. Crawford, who is a friend of hers. Mrs. Crawford told Mr. Crawford."

"Mr. Crawford is dean of your school and he called me in for a conference so that he could tell *me*," Mrs. Dillman concluded sadly. Ever since that "talk," Mrs. Dillman suffered a fit of nerves every time Franny opened a book. Only the evening before, Franny had overheard her mother say *sotto voce* over the teacups to her father, "She's reading again, Howard. It's an affliction. She doesn't just read. She hurtles herself into books and glues herself to the pages."

Franny didn't think this was a fair description. She didn't "glue" herself to pages. She didn't read to get stuck. She read to live, to love, to feel. She had *been* Jane Eyre. As Jane she had had the most rapturous month following Mr. Crawford, waiting to bump into him in the corridors at school, trailing him around the neighborhood, realizing to her delight that his wife was seldom around and that a sallow, elderly woman took care of their house and six-year-old son. She had deduced that Mrs. Crawford, like Mrs. Rochester in *Jane Eyre*, was mad, and that the lady was her keeper. As it turned out, Mrs. Crawford was getting her master's degree in psychiatric social work at Columbia. The old lady was her mother, who had come to help out by looking after the house and child.

Mrs. Dillman sat down at the foot of Franny's bed and began to smooth the coverlet. "Perhaps it would be better if you read a different kind of book," she mused. "This dramatic material sets your imagination to work at such a fevered pitch. Perhaps you shouldn't read the Brontës."

"Oh, don't say that." Franny put her hands over her ears. How she hated the idea of Authors and Authoresses. She could hardly bring herself to look at their photographs on the backs of books. She didn't like the thought of them meddling in what she believed to be Real Life.

"At any rate, reading in the closet is unhealthy." Mrs. Dillman sighed.

Franny read in the closet by flashlight because reading in the closet made everything more intense. Everything but the light. Being at Thornfield Hall with Jane Eyre or at Netherfield with Elizabeth Bennet in *Pride and Prejudice* was better than anything that happened in her Daily Life. She flopped into her desk chair.

"I really don't know what you're talking about," she said dully.

Mrs. Dillman got up from the bed and kissed the top of Franny's head. "I have to go to the market for a few things," she said in her brightest voice. "Why don't you practice a little while I'm gone. Wilson is staying late for science club, and Grace is working on the yearbook, so you've got the whole house to yourself. I'll be back by five. Put the casserole in the oven and set it at three-fifty."

"Okay," Franny said.

She went downstairs with her mother. On the wall of the stairwell, framed and hung like steps, were the gold-medal award to Grace Dillman for excellence in history, and The Scholastic Achievement Award to Wilson Dillman for accomplishment in biology. At the bottom of the stairs was something called a "wall hanging" (because that's where it was) by Frances Dillman. She had made it at the "Happy Days Are Here Again" Day Camp some seven years before. It had in it, among other things, bits of uncooked macaroni and Coca-Cola bottle caps. "Isn't it original?" Mrs. Dillman would always say of it to guests. "See the clever way she used these unusual found bits and pieces." Franny knew there was nothing found or original about it. The counselors had given them the macaroni and Coca-Cola bottle caps. It was the day camp's way of making art supplies out of garbage. As far as she was concerned there was more garbage than art in her "wall hanging." However, she knew perfectly well she had never gotten a gold medal, and until one came her way she was to be represented upon the family wall with a piece of framed trash.

When they got to the bottom of the stairs, Mrs. Dillman put on her coat and scarf and picked up her purse. "By the way, sweetheart, I think you've had enough chips for the time being."

"The time being?" What did that mean?

"You know, sweetie, it's such awful food for the figure."

"I love chips," Franny said. "Are you asking me not to eat them?" She couldn't believe it. *Jane Eyre* and her favorite food all at the same time.

Mrs. Dillman backed off. "No, dear. Just do watch out for them."

She went into the living room. Her mother was a puzzling person, she decided. How did one watch out for food? It wasn't an oncoming train or a thunderstorm. You couldn't have a "food watch." Food, along with books, was the best thing in the world. Put them together at the back of the closet and *Ahhhhh*.

She settled slowly on the piano bench, waiting for the slam of the front door which would mean she was alone. The door slammed. Franny breathed deeply. Drawing her plump person up in a dancer-like movement, she gracefully opened the book of music before her. Immediately she decided she was Jane Eyre in the scene of her second meeting with Mr. Rochester, when he asks her to play for him.

"Do you play?" he had said.

"A little," Jane had replied, not dreaming that her master, solemn, gruff Mr. Rochester, already had fallen hopelessly in love with her.

Franny began the Mozart piece. A pure and serious Jane-like smile played upon her lips. She swayed over the keys, picturing the elegant room at Thornfield Hall, letting its atmosphere drench and suffuse her till the ordinary living room of the Dillmans' house was obliterated, picturing Mr. Rochester's hot, passionate gaze upon her, picturing herself, humble serious Jane, playing until he should stop her with his "enough." She heard the front door open and close. She played a little faster, her fingers skimming of their own accord over the keys. She heard the chairs in the kitchen scrape, the cupboards rattle. She played louder, drowning out the sounds, arching her neck back for the allegro movement.

"Hey, fatso," Wilson yelled in, "did you finish the boysenberry ice cream?"

Franny slammed her fingers on the keys. "I hate you," she hissed.

Wilson appeared unperturbed in the doorway. "You ate *my* portion that I saved from last night for today. You eat up everything. You eat everything in sight, and it shows."

"I don't hate you," Franny corrected herself. "That's too generous an emotion. You are not worthy of consideration."

"I am your brother," Wilson said. "And if I am not careful I'll die of malnutrition, thanks to you." He left the room.

For the second time that afternoon her mood had been shattered. She went into the kitchen, the place where she always mended shattered moods. She was suddenly so hungry she thought she'd faint. Wilson was sitting at the table going through a box of Mallomars. He held on to it with one hand while loading his mouth with the other.

"I won't take it away from you," Franny said contemptuously. "I have no interest in those sordid things." She opened the refrigerator, took out a carrot stick, and strode from the room, head high.

When she finally heard Wilson leave the kitchen, she returned quietly. To her dismay, the empty Mallomar box was in the garbage. She took two slices of bread and covered them with mayonnaise and ketchup. She was in the middle of arranging hunks of cheese over the bread when Mrs. Dillman returned with fresh supplies. Franny watched her unpack the groceries. She waited with bated breath for toasted cashews or barbecued plantain chips, Oreos, or Vienna Fingers, but her mother's selection was unusually dull. An assortment of nutritional staples moved quickly from table to shelf.

When she had finished unpacking, Mrs. Dillman said, "I bought something just for you, Franny." She handed a small parcel across the table. Inside there were four paperback books. "The lady at the Book Nook recommended these," her mother said. "They deal with the everyday problems of boys and girls your age. Why not try them? She says they are realistic and true to life."

"Okay," said Franny. She opened the cover of the top book. "I'll take a look."

And that was when the trouble really began.

Franny went up to her room with the new books. She sat down on her bed, stuffed a pillow behind her back, and began to read the first page of *It's Okay to Cry a Lot*. She knew immediately that this was not a closet book.

It began:

"My name is Samantha. Before my mom had her nervous breakdown and went to the hospital, she called me Simsam. But she was the only person to call me that. My Dad calls me Sambox. Or at least he did before he split six months ago with his girl friend. Her name is Daisy. I guess you can figure by now that I have a pretty complicated home life. I do.

Sort of. Me and Mom and Dad and my frog
Suki lived in this big apartment on Central
Park West. We really never could afford it.
My grandfather paid for it. Right now I live
with my grandparents in New Jersey. Until
six months ago my life was not perfect, but it
was okay. Then everything happened at once.
I turned fourteen, Dad left with Daisy, Mom
cracked up, I got these zits all over my forehead and hair all over my legs that I have to
shave off *twice* a week. Also I cried a lot so
my eyes were always swollen."

Franny put the book down for a moment. Her
head reeled. She picked up the other books one at
a time and read the copy on the backs of them. *For
Keeps* was about Pammy who at eighteen has her
first affair and whose best friend Cindy has an
abortion. *Lord, Can I Call You Collect?* was about
Melissa, whose parents get a divorce; and *Life Goes
On, I Suppose* was about Nell, whose mother was
never married, not even to her father, who has dia-
betes. Nell has hypoglycemia.

Franny then went back to Samantha. She read
without stopping until it was time to go downstairs
and help with preparations for dinner.

Four days later, at twelve-fifteen in the morning,
Franny finished the last of the books her mother
had brought her. She had not practiced the piano,
done any homework, or gotten a full night's sleep
in four days. She had used every spare minute to

read. She placed *Life Goes On, I Suppose* on top of the other three books on her night table and turned off the light. Then she folded her arms behind her head and gazed up at her ceiling, thinking. What on earth had her mother meant when she said, "They deal with the everyday problems of girls and boys your age"? It was true that the girls she had just read about were not governesses in England in the middle part of the last century, and that they lived in modern suburbs or cities. However, it was also true that Franny didn't have a single problem in common with them. Not that she had no problems. She had problems all right, but they were limp, second-rate, grade-B numbers compared with the first-rate, class-A problems she had just read about.

There was one thing she could have in common with her new heroines, and that was a journal. Every one of them kept a journal. Franny decided that she would start a journal the very next day. Comforted by the thought that she would have something in common with Pammy, Nell, Melissa, and Samantha, she fell asleep.

At four o'clock the following afternoon, as soon as she got home from school, Franny went into the kitchen to make up a tray. Her mother had taken to hiding special foods behind the maple syrup can in back of the refrigerator. It was a simple-minded move which Franny had figured out weeks earlier. She reached back behind the can and was re-

warded with a small jar of herring in cream sauce.
No doubt this was intended for her parents' cock-
tail hour. As it was full to the brim, one missing
fillet and a few curls of onion would surely not be
missed. She carefully removed the topmost herring
and then smoothed the surface of cream to make
it look flat. Herring required rye bread. Rye bread
required root beer. Root beer required a scoop of
vanilla ice cream. And so, one thing led to another,
and before long her tray was filled to the edges.
She carried it up to her room.

When the snack was finished, Franny carefully
washed and dried her hands. As her mother had
advised, she had kept away from the chips. She
settled before her desk, opened a fresh notebook,
clicked her ballpoint pen, and wrote, "Wednesday,
Oct. 22."

She stared at the notebook and in one distressing
moment realized that she had nothing to write.
She wrote, "Nothing. Absolutely nothing happens
around here to me or anyone else. Nothing goes
on. I live in a dull backwater of an exciting city.
The twentieth century has not penetrated this
pocket of the Bronx. My folks are still married to
each other. They don't even fight. Though she is
seventeen, my sister Grace has not had an affair.
She hardly goes out with guys. If she did, she
wouldn't tell me about it. My brother Wilson is an
equal zero. At fourteen he should be a seething
caldron of erotic impulses. He should be climbing

the walls. Instead he sublimates with math and science. He doesn't even have acne."

Franny put down her pen and stared out the window that faced her desk. Her mother was raking leaves in the backyard. It had been a long, brilliant fall. Though it was the end of October, the leaves were just falling. Mrs. Dillman made small heaps of them at regular intervals. Completely absorbed in her work and her private thoughts, her expression was preoccupied. Franny watched her carefully. Her cheeks were pink from exertion and the chilly air. Her dark curly hair was tied back with a piece of thick orange wool. Though small, Mrs. Dillman had a strong, wiry body. The mothers in the books Franny had been reading fought with their husbands, wanted to find themselves, cracked up and/or treated their daughters' problems with great seriousness. None of these interesting activities had occurred to Mrs. Dillman. Franny tapped her pen impatiently on her desk and pulled at her lip. What was she to do?

Then it came to her. Just because nothing had happened in her life didn't mean she couldn't *make* something happen. She wrote, "I will make something happen." Immediately another thought came to her. Was it possible that things *were* happening which she had not noticed? Things that were just as exciting as anything she had read about? This idea changed everything. "I will make it my business to unearth the events that must be quietly erupting in my family," she wrote. "I will unearth them, explode them, observe them, and record them. I will go at least two steps further than any girl I've read about lately."

◈◈◈◈◈◈◈◈◈◈◈◈◈◈◈◈

2

"Where is Dad?" said Franny at six-thirty when her mother called her in to set the table.

"He had a meeting," Mrs. Dillman said.

"Oh?"

"What's that 'oh'?" Mrs. Dillman sounded amused.

"Just 'oh.'" Franny arranged the plates on the table. "What's the meeting about?"

"I don't know, dear."

"Didn't Dad tell you?"

"I didn't ask."

She folded the napkins. "You two don't communicate very much, do you?"

Mrs. Dillman looked up from the pot she was stirring. "What makes you say that?"

"He didn't tell you about the meeting. You didn't ask."

"No, I didn't."

"That's what I mean."

Mrs. Dillman gave her a funny look. "*You* ask him when he comes home, Franny, since you're so curious."

"Okay." She set four glasses around the stripped-oak kitchen table.

Grace Dillman came into the kitchen to check on bread she had put in the oven. Grace was an excellent bread baker, gymnast, and student.

"I assumed we were eating in the kitchen tonight," Franny said.

"Yes, of course, dear," Mrs. Dillman said.

"Why do you say 'of course'?" said Franny. "When Dad is home we eat in the dining room."

"That is true. He prefers it, and five is a bit cramped in the kitchen."

"But it's more work for *you*, going back and forth."

"I suppose it is."

Franny hoped that she had planted a seed. But her mother didn't seem to have caught on. Certainly it was true that her father's sense of decorum involved her mother in making a greater effort. They only ate frozen foods and take-out dinners when he was away or at a meeting. When he was home it was The Dining Room and Home-Cooked Meals, and Candles and Wine. This very situation had let to the breakup of one of her new heroine's parents' marriage. That and the fact that the girl's mother had to "find herself." Franny had a new thought.

"Have you found yourself, Mom?" she asked slowly.

Mrs. Dillman cackled. "I wasn't lost."

"No, you know what I mean. I mean, do you ever want to go back to school and take courses?"

Mrs. Dillman smiled at Franny reassuringly. "Frances," she said in her soothing voice, "I was thirty when I got married and thirty-two when Grace was born. I had years to find myself. I like my life. I enjoy all my jobs." She patted Franny's shoulder as if to dismiss her daughter's concern.

Mrs. Dillman had gone back to teaching math at the Bronx Community College.

Grace glanced up from the oven. Every time she looked up she had to shove her glasses back up onto her nose, and her hair out of her face. "Poor us, Fran, our Ma does not appear to require assertiveness training, consciousness raising, or career counseling. What are we to do with the lazy thing?"

"I may need a retirement community one day," Mrs. Dillman warned.

"I remain unconvinced," Franny said, refusing to join in on their joke. None of her heroines joked. They were distinctly unfunny. They took life very, very seriously, as if being an "adolescent" was like having an illness, and one needed to speak of the entire thing in a hushed and reverent tone.

If ever there was any humor, it was the sort that brought a lump to your throat, not the sort that made you laugh out loud. Her mother and her sister were uncooperative and rude, to say the least.

"All I was saying was that just because of *him*, Mom has to drag everything into the dining room and plan feasts for dinner every night with candles and wine."

"Just because of *him?*" Mrs. Dillman's smile left her face. She put both hands on her hips. "Just because of *him* we maintain a bit of style in this household, Missy. Remember the word, style. We have not come all this way to suck frozen peas out of paper boxes and chew hash out of tins in the galley. Such scenes do not strike me as homey or charmingly casual. If from time to time we dine informally on packaged dinners, we do so because for the most part we live like civilized people with standards."

There they were, Franny thought. A hopeless family.

"You can't seriously want to eat pig style, old thing," said Grace in her new affected English voice.

"I seriously wish I had an interesting life," Franny said, "with an interesting family who did fascinating things."

"*Tant pis*," said Grace, making her French face.

Franny settled for twisting the dinner napkins into weird, unpleasant shapes.

Wilson came into the kitchen. "What are you doing to my napkin?" he squawked.

"Making it into a phallus, you lunkhead."

Nothing. No blush, no perspiration, nothing. Maybe he didn't know what a phallus was.

"My, how your vocabulary has expanded," Gracie remarked, and the telephone rang.

"For you." Mrs. Dillman passed the receiver to Grace.

"Hi," Grace began.

Franny stopped twisting napkins and sat down to watch her sister. But Grace pulled the long cord after her, turned her back, and went into the pantry. It was only a visual trick. Franny could hear every word.

"My dear, that is *too* much," she heard Grace say in the English voice. "Doesn't he know? I mean, I know, and you know, how come he doesn't know?"

Franny had never paid much attention to her sister's phone conversations before. They were mainly conducted with a very peculiar girl named Hyacinth Nungazer, who had a passionate yearning to be the greatest soprano of her time. Hyacinth always gave the impression of being on an enormous stage. All her gestures were large, as was her voice. She was immersed in her music, her drama, her Italian, and her ballet. She referred to her voice in the third person. "The Nungazer sound is stronger this year," she would say, swinging out both arms and expanding her impressive chest to

indicate strength. Gracie got a big charge out of
Hyacinth, but she liked her too. They spent hours
on the telephone. It had never occurred to Franny
that they talked anything but nonsense. At least
it hadn't occurred to her till now. Since reading
For Keeps, which was about an eighteen-year-old
high-school senior who has a love affair and an
orgasm, Franny suddenly thought of her sister as
a gold mine of romantic, if not pornographic, po-
tential.

"I mean, I know you know he knows, how come
he doesn't know you know I know."

"Perketh up thine ears," Franny said to herself.
"All this drivel could be solid platinum if only I
get the key."

"He said I said you said they said *that?*" Hilarious laughter. "No!"

"Oh, shoot," Wilson said to his mother, waving
at the pantry. "She's verging on womanhood."

"We Dillmans and Blatts are late bloomers," said
Mrs. Dillman.

"When does a late bloomer qualify as a retard?"

"I don't like remarks like that."

It occurred to Franny that her mother was
snippy and tensed up about something. Life was
improving; if only one looked, one might find the
stuff of a readable journal.

"Hey, Mom." Gracie opened the pantry door.
"Can Hyacinth come over for dinner?"

"Surely," Mrs. Dillman said. "There's plenty of
food."

"Should I reset the table in the dining room?" said Franny.

"No, don't bother." Mrs. Dillman was leafing through her cookbook.

So five was suddenly not "cramped" in the kitchen. How she deludes herself, Franny thought. Her head is full of holes. Franny committed this image to memory for later use in her journal.

Hyacinth arrived a few minutes later. Her entrance was operatic, as usual. She was wearing a brand-new cape, which was part of the reason she had to come over. They were all to admire and comment on this purple velvet thing that she had dredged out of the back room of the Hospital Thrift Shop.

"Downtown they're getting seventy-five dollars for these, it's a genuine antique," Hyacinth said, twirling her five feet ten inches so that the moth-eaten, camphory folds swelled out like a mushroom cap. "Isn't it divine? I feel like Manon, or Lucia di Lammermoor. I love the way it slims me."

"It's very interesting," said Mrs. Dillman diplomatically.

"Oh, I adore it," Gracie cried. "It's perfect, absolutely perfect. If I had to choose the thing that you were born to wear, it would be that, Hyacinth. Can I try it on?"

Hyacinth whipped off the cape and handed it to Grace in a cloud of dust. "On you it's wasted," she said. "You don't have to cover anything."

"Cover anything?" Mrs. Dillman protested.

"Hyacinth, you're not heavy. You have nothing to conceal."

Franny caught a look exchanged between Hyacinth and Grace.

"That's your opinion, Mrs. D.," Hyacinth sighed. "But I am out of style with these hips, not to mention my bosom. I do not have an American Girl body, let's face it. Mother says I should stop pretending and dress cleverly as a large woman."

"Nonsense," Mrs. Dillman said. "You're statuesque . . . Junoesque . . . Rubenesque."

"Look at me." Grace had put on the cape and was in a transport over it, draping it this way and that, sucking in her cheeks like a model, thrusting the sooty ends of the garment over one shoulder.

"Drivel," Wilson said and went back up to his room.

"I must see myself." Grace, with Hyacinth behind her, went out to the front hall where there was a full-length mirror.

Mrs. Dillman smiled and shook her head. "She's really not heavy. She has nothing to hide."

"How do you know?" Franny said.

"What's that supposed to mean?"

"I don't know," Franny shrugged. Till that very moment, she didn't know, but something had come to her. It was right out of *For Keeps*. Pammy, the heroine Franny liked best, had taught her a thing or two about capes and cloaks and loose clothes to hide an expanding shape. There it was. If you knew enough to look, you could find.

In a few minutes Grace and Hyacinth returned
to the kitchen without the cape. Wilson was sum-
moned for dinner. Franny noticed that he had
shaved the disreputable stubble off his upper lip
and chin and replaced it with two bloody nicks
adorned by little plumes of toilet paper. He smelled
sickeningly of Vitalis. Something interesting there.
Also, he seemed to make an effort to stand as close
to Hyacinth as possible while they were deciding
where to sit. Just as Grace was removing her bread
from the oven, the front door banged shut and
Mr. Dillman's voice filled the house.

"Surprise! Meeting canceled. Is there enough for
me?"

"Always, my love," Mrs. Dillman called back.

Without waiting to be asked, Franny began to
stack up the dishes, silver, and napkins to take into
the dining room. Hyacinth helped, in her fashion.
Hyacinth, who could make large dramatic gestures,
was hopeless at small, practical ones. She could
beat her chest and wring her hands, but she could
not carry two plates and a spoon without dropping
one of them. Franny watched her nervously. The
serving spoons clattered to the floor before she
got to the dining room.

"Gosh, I don't know what's the matter with me."
Hyacinth stooped to the floor.

Franny noticed that her hands were shaking.
Was she in a state because of Mr. Dillman? Was it
Mr. Dillman's return home? More observation re-

quired on this. Hyacinth was a very passionate person.

Soon the table in the dining room was set. Mr. Dillman had hung up his coat and gone upstairs to wash.

Gracie was slicing her bread in a worshipful way. Mrs. Dillman was adding sherry to the frozen dinner in a last-ditch effort to class it up for the *man*, Franny supposed. When Mr. Dillman came downstairs, he too was fragrant with some fresh application of cologne. He rubbed his hands together, beaming a warm smile upon them all.

"What a treat to be home with you instead of at that dreary meeting," he said. "And a special treat to find *you* here, Hyacinth, dear."

"Oh, Mr. Dillman, you're always so gallant." Hyacinth pronounced gallant in a French way and curved all five feet ten in a graceful curtsy.

"What heavenly smells," Mr. Dillman said.

"Let's hope." Mrs. Dillman brought in the casserole in which she had combined three separate packages of Mrs. Peter's Frozen Stew. She set the casserole on the side table. It was Franny's opinion that these frozen dinners were far superior to her mother's big, start-from-scratch *New York Times Cook Book* numbers. She would observe her father carefully to see if he was smart enough to realize what he'd been missing.

Mr. Dillman was a slender, stooped man with a kindly, flat face which featured what Mrs. Dillman called a strong chin and what Franny called a lantern jaw. Franny thought her father looked like an old piece of good furniture. Frayed in spots, but sturdy and comfortable. Tonight he was especially comfortable.

"Oh, the joys of not having to sit through endless meetings," he said, filling wineglasses for himself, his wife, Grace, and Hyacinth. "Hyacinth, you seem to be especially blooming."

"Daddy, you should see the fantastic cape Hyacinth unearthed at a thrift shop," Gracie gushed.

"I'd love to see it. Will you model it for us, Hyacinth?"

"Not at dinner, Mr. Dillman," Hyacinth protested, both hands flying to her bosom. "Not at dinner, please."

"With dessert, then," Mr. Dillman said. "A treat with the sweet."

Something was going on here. Something was happening between her father and Hyacinth, Franny thought. Could she call it a flirtation? She observed Wilson carefully. His head was down; sublimating with food, he was eating so that his mouth nearly touched the rim of the plate. He was withdrawn from the jocularity at the table. Equally withdrawn, Franny noted, was her mother, who spooned food onto dishes in an intent, preoccupied manner. When Wilson looked up, there was an expression of suffering suffusing his face. The look was directed at Hyacinth's bosom. "Are we out of food?" he asked. There was plenty going on, all right.

Mrs. Dillman poured some more wine, and there was much comment on the taste of the drink.

"It's both young and wise," Hyacinth said of the wine. "In a word, sprightly."

"Hyacinth, you are really too much." Mrs. Dillman laughed.

Though she laughed, she didn't fool Franny for a minute. There was real criticism in her voice. No one else was noticing anything. They all kept talking and laughing and eating and having what would have appeared to an outsider as a high old time.

When Mrs. Dillman got up to clear the dinner plates, Mr. Dillman reminded Hyacinth that it was time for the fashion show.

Giggling all the way from the dining room to the front hall, Grace and Hyacinth suddenly fell quiet. As Mrs. Dillman returned with a tray of coffee and cups and saucers, Hyacinth appeared dramatically framed in the dining-room archway, wrapped in her cape. She raised both arms and began without any warning to sing Mimi's aria from the first act of *La Bohème*, the one where she looks for a key. Great big Hyacinth pretending to be little tubercular Mimi, seamstress of the Paris garret, was more than Franny could endure. She put her napkin over her face and, under her mother's glare, tried to make her hysteria sound like a choking fit.

When Hyacinth had finished, Mr. and Mrs. Dillman and Grace applauded. "Hyacinth," Mr. Dillman said, "that was lovely. Your diction, your control of the upper register, and your vibrato were on a professional level."

"Thank you, Mr. Dillman." Hyacinth entered the room meekly and took her seat.

"You looked and sounded like Mimi," said Mrs. Dillman.

"The cape helped me."

"The cape is made for you," Grace said.

"And it will give her room to grow in," Mr. Dillman winked at Hyacinth.

"I wonder if you mean that figuratively, Mr. D.," Hyacinth said.

"Any way you like, Miss N."

They all laughed.

Room to grow in? Franny heard the words and the laughter and then *snap*. The story was clear.

Hyacinth was pregnant.

Mr. Dillman knew.

Was he responsible?

Wilson loved Hyacinth.

This was a romantic triangle.

Gracie knew.

Mrs. Dillman guessed.

And Franny Dillman, who had started the day with nothing at all, had lots of things to put down in her journal.

3

〰〰〰〰〰〰〰〰〰〰〰〰〰〰

Every Saturday morning, Franny and her friend
Rosy Shuloff went to the Manhattan School of
Music. They took piano, theory, and choral singing. Usually when classes were over at noon, they
would have lunch and go to a museum or a movie.
On the Friday of that week, before she went to
bed, Franny sat up at her desk writing in her
journal.

"Friday, Oct. 24. Now that I have the key, so
many things are falling into place. Tomorrow
Gracie and Hyacinth are going downtown. They
say they want to shop and visit the Diaghilev show
at the Met, but they kept whispering and giggling
on the phone. It's obvious that they plan to do
something secretive. I have a pretty good idea of
what it is. If my guess is right *it* is a visit to the

Margaret Sanger Clinic to get abortion and birth control information." Franny paused to thumb through her dog-eared copy of *For Keeps.* She turned to the chapter in which Pammy goes to the Margaret Sanger Clinic, is interviewed, examined, and given the Pill. "I do not plan to go into the building," Franny decided in her journal. "I'll wait outside and then, when I see them come out, pretend to be passing by. That way they'll know that I'm aware of what's going on. I think it will help. They'll have one less person to pretend for."

She paused, as a problem had presented itself. "What will I do with Rosy?" Should she tell Rosy? Technically, Rosy was her best friend, but Rosy took everything very seriously. When she had been younger and crueler, Franny had actually clocked the length of time it took for her to make Rosy cry over some invented story involving either a horse or a dog. Now Rosy cried over rodents, cats, and babies as well. "I better ditch her," Franny wrote and closed her journal.

She was tired. It had been an exhausting few days. Since Wednesday, only two days before, when she had first made her breakthrough observations, so many thoughts and feelings had been erupting within her that she could hardly keep track of them. Her imagination was at a fever pitch. Watching her mother, watching Wilson, watching her father, trailing Grace and Hyacinth, trying to make sense of the many things they said was an almost impossible task, combined with school work and her own social life. Everything she had observed in the last two days had strengthened and confirmed her first conclusions. This was unraveling into a story with tremendous implications. That much was clear, no matter what surface confusions might obscure the picture.

She stretched, turned off her desk lamp, turned on her night-table light, turned off the overhead, and climbed into bed and opened *For Keeps*. She gave it a fast review before going to sleep. As she closed the book she realized that she was unbelievably lucky to have discovered, under her very nose, a plot and characters right out of the books she had been reading.

"Are you feeling all right, Franny?" Mrs. Dillman said at breakfast the next morning. "You're not eating."

"I'm okay."

"I have never seen you leave a waffle untouched," Mrs. Dillman marveled.

"I think I ought to watch my weight," Franny said, patting her midsection.

"Now, that's not a bad idea," said Mrs. Dillman quickly, as if she had been waiting months for the chance to agree with it.

Franny was taken aback. "Do you think I'm fat?"

"I didn't say that, dear. I simply agreed that you might want to watch what you eat."

"I said, do you think I'm fat?"

"I didn't say that." Mrs. Dillman looked upset.

"I think I'll eat what I like." Franny stuffed the whole waffle into her mouth with her fingers. She was suddenly ravenous. "I'm only thirteen. I'm growing."

"You can say that again," Wilson said.

"What's that supposed to mean?" she said through full cheeks.

"Just what I said." Wilson met her glare. "You're growing wider and wider. If you ever wore anything but those baggy overalls it would be all over for you, Frances."

"Don't be hurtful," said Mrs. Dillman.

"But it's true. She eats like a horse and she's starting to look like a pony."

"Stop it, Wilson." Mr. Dillman came into the kitchen in his robe. "That sort of remark isn't helpful."

"It helps him," Franny said in a superior voice. "Being mean to me is an outlet for him." She stood up and marched out of the kitchen. In the front hall she cautiously approached the full-length mirror. She always approached it cautiously. Otherwise it could give her a nasty surprise. Such as if she was thinking of something else and suddenly she saw reflected this very chubby person who was supposed to be herself. In her mind she was a very slender person, and so she would very quickly have to forget what she had seen in the mirror. Sometimes she would come up to it again, sucking in her gut and showing a three-quarter view with both arms pinned to her sides. It was an awkward

position, but one in which she was a much less
chubby-looking person with very nice black hair
and beautiful skin and pink cheeks and lovely
green eyes. Actually she would look at her face and
avoid the rest. The rest was giving her problems.
She had been skinny for years while eating everything she liked. Suddenly a year ago her body had
betrayed her. It had puffed and developed and done
new and surprising things. She didn't like putting
names to the things. She didn't like to think about
them. One of them turned out to be "fat."

"Are you leaving soon, old girl?" Gracie called
from the top of the staircase.

"Yeah." Franny let her rib cage deflate with a
sigh. "I just have to get my books together and
then I pick up Rosy. Why?"

"I wonder if you could mail something for me."

"Sure." Franny went halfway up the steps to get
the envelope. "When are you and Hyacinth going
downtown?" she said.

"Not till noon."

"Oh, good."

"Why good?"

"I don't know." Franny shrugged. Suddenly
Grace was looking at her oddly. Her glasses were
halfway down her nose, and her blond hair fell
like a double curtain on either side of her brow.
She folded her arms over the front of her old
flannel nightgown.

"Are you okay, Franner?" she said. "You've been
funny for the last few days."

"I'm okay."

"Anytime you want to have a serious talk with me about . . . things, just ask. Will you?"

"Uh huh." She looked away, down the worn carpeted stairs.

"Thirteen isn't an easy year," Grace went on in a gentle, professional-counselor voice, "and you're such an imaginative, inventive sort of kid. I know you're going through a lot."

"Oh, bug off." Franny rushed downstairs. "I don't know what you're blubbering about."

Her mother was coming out of the kitchen. "Franny, I think you should take an umbrella. It looks overcast." She was fishing in her pocketbook. "Here are your tokens and some extra money for lunch. Please don't come home later than five. You know how I worry."

"I know, I know." She put on her jacket, picked up her books, tucked Gracie's letter into them, took the tokens and bills between her teeth and the umbrella under her arm. She opened the door.

"Pull yourself together a little, dear," her mother was saying as the door closed.

Rosy lived in an apartment house two blocks away. She was waiting outside stamping her feet as if it were cold. It wasn't cold; Franny knew it was Rosy's way of saying, "You're five minutes late and see how I'm suffering for you." In her red hands she held her music and a bag full of old rolls.

"Hi," Franny called. "You look cold."

"Oh, *I'm* not the one who's cold," Rosy chat-

tered. "But there's this bird in Mrs. Damson's yard
that stayed on too long, Franny. It didn't fly south
in time?" She always told things with a question
mark at the end. "And it stayed because Mrs.
Damson went to Utica to visit her son and the
bird is starving and freezing?"

"Uh huh."

"And so if you don't mind, it won't make us late
or take a minute, I'll just put a little food in Mrs.
Damson's yard." This was not a question, as Rosy
was already turning into Mrs. Damson's yard. A
fierce-looking grackle swooped down from a tree
onto the lawn.

"Holy cow," Franny said. "That's not a bird.
That's a horrible grackle. They don't go south.
They're non-migratory. They just converge by the
zillion on miles of corn and eat it up. Everybody
wants to kill them."

The grackle turned red, reptilian eyes filled with
hatred in her direction.

"How can you?" Rosy cried in horror. Then to
the bird she crooned, "Here, little darling. Here,
little love." She crumbled the rolls onto the ground.

"Little love?" Franny scoffed. "It's a dinosaur.
Look at it. They're grotesque birds. They don't
deserve to live."

"Fascist pig," Rosy muttered under her breath,
shaking out the bag, her eyes filling with tears.
"Nazi. Here, little sweetheart. Eat for your long
trip. You'll go to Florida. You'll make it."

"To Fort Lauderdale on the wing of a seven-forty-seven. Or maybe in the engine. It and its two zillion cousins. If they don't bring the plane down they'll eat every crop in sight."

Rosy had finished shaking out the last crumb. She folded up the bag and dusted her fingers on her coat. She followed Franny out of the yard. "Really, Fran, I know you don't mean to be cruel and heartless, it's just your act, but sometimes you go too far. Even for you."

When Rosy got preachy, Franny found her particularly hard to take. She decided to change the subject. "Have you read *For Keeps?*"

"Oh, no," Rosy said. "My mother doesn't approve of the sex in those books. She thinks they would be hard for me to handle. Have you read them?"

Franny was shocked into temporary silence. Sex? Hard to handle? Not any of those books at any time had done for her what *Jane Eyre* had done. Not once had her insides simply melted in a divine sensation of ecstasy. Not once. What did Mrs. Shuloff mean? Words like pregnant? Abortion? Orgasm? They had to do with information, not feelings. Still, she had to admit she found them titillating.

Franny made a note to herself to use titillating words in her own journal. She liked the idea of writing something that Mrs. Shuloff would find hard for Rosy to handle. This reminded her of her day's plans.

"I can't have lunch and go to the movies today," Franny said. "I have some important private business to attend to."

"You what?" Rosy looked shocked. "What kind of business?"

"I just said, private."

"Oh." They walked the three blocks to the subway in silence. A cloud of hurt feelings hung in the air between them.

On the subway platform Franny said, "I wish you wouldn't be angry about this."

"I am not angry," Rosy said angrily.

"Just because every single Saturday we do something together doesn't mean that once in a while we can't separate. You should feel good about it. You can do something on your own, too, for a change."

"I don't have anything to do," Rosy said so forlornly that Franny nearly capitulated and let her in on the whole thing. But when she saw Rosy's eyes begin to moisten with self-pity, she changed her mind.

The subway ride was too noisy to bother talking, and once they got to school they were too busy. At noon, when classes ended, Franny didn't wait for Rosy at all. She grabbed her coat and books and ran out.

She knew from reading *For Keeps* that there was a group appointment at the clinic with a social worker and a doctor. The meeting was at two forty-five. One thing about *For Keeps*—it left very

little to the imagination. Two forty-five on the
nose.

Franny decided that she would eat lunch near
the clinic so that she would have plenty of time.
She tried to make her hamburger and french fries
last, but the counterman at the luncheonette began
to stare at her and wipe the Formica around her
plate and make impatient sounds when she helped
herself to another free pickle. She munched on the
pickle and looked around her. What was she doing
here? Suddenly she felt all her certainty and con-
fidence sucked away, as if a strong vacuum cleaner
had passed over that part of her that made her
Frances Dillman. She was left feeling wobbly and
wondering who she was.

The first time she had experienced this calami-
tous sensation was two years before, in the dressing
room of the Fashion Box Booteek. She had gone
to the store with her mother for new clothes (having outgrown everything she had) and had learned
she could no longer wear Young Miss sizes and
was too "chubby," according to the saleslady, for
the preteens. The saleslady had also said, "Who'd
ever think that Gracie's kid sister would have such
a problem?" Franny had insisted on a pair of pre-
teen jeans. She was standing in front of the mirror
squeezed into a pair of pants she was certain had
been mismarked. Her mother had just said, "Do
you think you can sit down in those, dear?" when
the awful hollow feeling came over her. The invisible vacuum cleaner had simply sucked her

entire sense of well-being and certainty away.
"Who am I? How did I get here?" was all that was
left.

"Well," her mother had said, "you're no size ten,
that much is for sure. Take those things off before
one of you pops."

That was the first time. Since then the sensation
would overtake her from out of the blue. She had
learned to dispel it by telling herself exactly who
she was and what she was doing.

"Frances," she began to herself, "you are involved in an incredibly important mission. You
are on the brink of it. Now snap out of this. You
must track down Grace and Hyacinth for their
own good." She snapped out of it and regained
her composure.

She paid her bill and left the luncheonette. She
had looked up the exact address of the clinic in
the telephone directory. It was just where it was
supposed to be in an office building on Second
Avenue.

Across the street from the clinic building there
was a modern church, made of dun-colored brick
in irregular funnel shapes. These funnels were in-
terspersed with windows that had been designed
to look as if they had been cracked. There were
cement planters outside the church in which trees
leaned at angles. It was behind one of these planters that Franny decided to wait.

A thin drizzle began to fall. The shoes she had
siliconed last winter were no longer waterproof.

The tree in the planter shed thick drops on her head. She remembered that she had left her umbrella at the luncheonette. A woman came out of the church and gave her a long funny look. She crossed the street to wait in the doorway of an antique shop. At two thirty there was still no sign of Gracie or Hyacinth. By two forty-five the man inside the antique shop had been glaring at her for several minutes, and the lost feeling was coming back. Also, she had to use the bathroom. She decided to go into the building. In the lobby she read the directory and then took the elevator up to the fourth floor. She stepped into a bright, pleasant waiting room. Two receptionists sat at a desk. Quickly Franny searched the orange couches and chairs for Grace and Hyacinth. They were not there.

"Excuse me, could you direct me to the ladies' room?" She kept her eyes down.

"To your left and through those double doors," one of the women said, as if nothing at all were going on.

Franny realized while she was in the ladies' room that her sister could have slipped into the building at that very moment and that the whole miserable afternoon might have been wasted. With relief she decided to go home.

"Franny, dear, why on earth did you ditch poor Rosy Shuloff? She's called three times this afternoon, asking if you got home yet. She said she was worried."

"That's just like her," Franny said. "Actually she was mad at me. I got tired of hanging around with her. I wanted a little time to myself. Is that so bad?"

"No, of course not, dear," Mrs. Dillman said sympathetically. "It just depends on how you put it to her."

"I put it straight."

"That's what I thought," Mrs. Dillman said, more to herself.

"Did Gracie get back yet?"

"No, I don't expect them for a while. They were going to the library at Lincoln Center and a few other places as well."

The telephone rang. It was Rosy.

"So," she said in the flat monotone that could drive Franny up the wall.

"So what?"

"So what did you do after you dumped me? What was the big deal you had to dump me for?"

Franny could imagine Rosy stooped over the telephone biting her nails delicately right down to the blood line or twisting the strands of pale hair into ropes, her dark, sad eyes squinting, either to see or hold back tears.

"I just wanted to attend to a few things by myself," Franny said.

"I see."

"You do?"

"I really don't."

"It's hard to explain."

"Try."

Franny thought for a moment of what she could say. "I can't," she finally mumbled. "At least not now."

"Okay, so g'by." Rosy hung up.

Franny sat staring at the telephone. How could she explain to Rosy what was happening? How could she tell her that at last her *real* life and her *book* life had come together in a glorious, fantastic way? How could she tell her that suddenly it had been her great fortune to find herself in the middle of a plot, surrounded by characters that exactly duplicated those in the books she had been reading?

For Franny was convinced that her life could be guided by all the rules of novels. She fervently believed that if she was clever and careful and quick, she would find in her daily life a plot complete with heroes, heroines, minor characters, dramatic situations, calamities, and coincidences that would structure themselves into the form of a novel similar to the ones she had just read. *If* she was diligent and observant and watched her every move, she *knew* that these moves would connect one to the other and would advance the plot of her Living Novel. How on earth could she have told all that to Rosy Shuloff?

After dinner she wrote, "October 25, Saturday. Even though I missed them, I think I was right.

They went to the clinic. They came home very excited and very secretive. When I asked about the library at Lincoln Center, they looked vague and then began to giggle. There was nothing at all said about the show at the Met. Hyacinth wore her cloak and Gracie her floppy hat and new boots with the fur trim. Gracie told Mom that Hyacinth has a crush on some tenor at the City Opera. Lincoln Center Library, hah.

"Question. How will Daddy react to this crush business? I must be sensitive to Wilson's pain when he learns that his feelings for Hyacinth are unrequited. What about Mother when she sees how involved Daddy is? I think Hyacinth is playing both my father and my brother for fools. I think that Gracie is her cohort. This is very French."

4

〰〰〰〰〰〰〰〰〰〰〰〰

Every year Franny had a different favorite subject. Anyone trying to get some idea of a drift in her interests would be at a loss. One year it was history, the next, science or math. Usually she detested English. This mystified her parents and her teachers. "I don't understand how anybody who loves to read as much as you do can perform so badly in English," Mrs. Dillman would say every time the report cards arrived. Franny tried to explain that she read books to *live*, not to analyze and pull apart and rearrange into tidy book reports.

In the eighth grade, however, for the first time she loved English best of all. English eight was taught by Mrs. Propper. Mrs. Propper had huge round brown eyes and a red Afro. She read books the way Franny did. She never asked her class to write a book report about "Three Ways in Which the Minor Characters Further the Development of the Plot." She asked, "How do you feel about Holden Caulfield? Do you know anybody like him? Have you ever felt like that?" She made the books they read come very close. Also the compositions she assigned got them involved. "Write about how you see yourself as a person of thirty." Franny could not imagine such a thing. But once she got started it was hard to stop. Mrs. Propper had told the class that she would accept journal entries in place of compositions.

After much debate with herself Franny decided to hand in her journal entry for Saturday, October twenty-fifth. She used initials instead of names and across the top she wrote CONFIDENTIAL.

The school Franny, Wilson, and Grace went to was private and large. Franny was in the middle school, sixth through ninth grade. Wilson and Grace were in the high school. The two divisions were housed in the same sprawling brick-and-stone building. The lower school was across the street.

Sometimes Franny would bump into Wilson or Grace, but not if she could help it. She avoided the fourth floor where Grace spent most of her time as the big-cheese editor of the yearbook. Also she avoided the science rooms where Wilson hung out long after classes were over. When she saw her brother and sister in their worlds, the vacuumed-away feeling of the Fashion Box Booteek dressing room would zap her between the eyes. She'd have to say to herself very fast, "I'm Frances Dillman and I have a secret mission and a secret life," over and over till the feeling went away.

Monday, October the twenty-seventh was not a good day. For one thing she was worried about handing in the journal entry, and for another she had met Gracie carrying a load of yearbook ad forms, flanked on both sides by senior boys who were falling all over themselves to help her. And for a third, she had seen Mr. Crawford.

He was standing at the end of the corridor waiting for the elevator. The minute she saw him Franny turned cold. He had his back to her, but she knew his four suits by heart, not to mention the particular slope of his rounded shoulders and the particular shape of his dark, brooding brow and the wonderful gestures of his muscular arms. Mr. Crawford, like Mr. Rochester in *Jane Eyre*, was of medium height and husky build. Like Mr. Rochester he had fierce black eyes, and like Mr. Rochester he had a small, sensitive, intelligent young woman to study his every mood. But Franny reminded herself painfully *all that was over*. It had led to problems which she had put behind her. Now she had found a whole new set of modern books with which to relate. Still, she realized, old feelings die hard. With a heart near bursting, she watched him turn toward her, as if he sensed her eyes on the back of his neck. He looked surprised to see her. The elevator door opened. He waved

nervously in her direction. "Hello there, Frances."
He seemed to lunge into the elevator and was gone
from her sight, but not her nervous system. She
could think of nothing else as she dreamily made
her way down the stairwell.

After that, Rosy Shuloff followed her into the
lunchroom with Mary Beth Blabbermouth Higgens
behind her.

"Say, I saw the 'confidential' on your paper,"
Rosy said. "What was it, a description of mysterious Saturday?"

Rosy was still hurt.

"It was confidential," Franny said, realizing in a
flash that she had made a big mistake handing in
that entry.

"Confidential?" Mary Beth's voice singsonged.
"Something new about mad, loony, licked-up Mrs.
Crawford?"

"Hah." Franny edged into a seat. But both of
them plunked down at the same table.

"I'd rather forget about all that," Franny muttered while opening a packet of potato chips with
her teeth. "It would never have amounted to anything if you hadn't blabbed to your mother."

Mary Beth was chastened.

"Anyway, I'm still not so sure about that household," Franny said darkly. "I think there was something funny going on. Mr. Crawford looks moody
and depressed to me."

"My mom says he's a big joker with his friends."

"I'd rather not hear about it." Franny sighed.

"I'm sure it's disgusting." She looked at Mary Beth and Rosy and got depressed. They were a group, all right. Not because they wanted to be or had picked each other out, but because they didn't fit in with anybody else. They had fallen together like loose change and lint and gum wrappers at the bottom of a pocket. They were secretly grateful to have one another, but also resentful because there had never been a question of choice. Since third grade they had eaten lunch together, no matter what. They each knew no one else would eat with them.

"Reeling back to Saturday," Rosy said. "What did you do?"

"Confidential," Franny said.

"Oh, come on, seriously."

"Seriously."

"Okay then, I'll guess." She stopped chewing and looked at the ceiling. "You followed Alan Nungazer to the library."

"Followed Alan Nungazer?" Franny repeated. "Even as low jest, that is very low."

Alan was Hyacinth's brother. He was as withdrawn as his sister was extroverted. He was in the ninth grade. Once, years before, Hyacinth and Grace had taken both Franny and Alan to a kiddie movie and for a soda afterward because they thought it was a "cute" idea. From then on Alan and Franny had nothing to do with one another.

"If you didn't follow Alan Nungazer, did you go back to following Mr. Crawford?"

"I'm through with Mr. Crawford and you, too," Franny snarled, "if you don't cut it out."

"Will you ditch me again this Saturday? I just want to know," Rosy said. There was egg salad on the end of her nose. She was a sloppy eater.

"No, I won't ditch you," Franny decided, to her own regret. That bit of egg salad had turned the trick. It was more pathetic than crying.

Later, when she got home and it was technically time for her to practice the piano, she could not find her book. She spent fifteen minutes of her practice time looking for it and gave up. She did a few exercises and one piece from memory before going into the kitchen to check things out.

"Hi," Gracie said. She was pounding away on a mound of dough. The telephone rang. Franny took it. A woman asked for "a Grace Dillman." Franny handed the phone to her sister with a shrug.

"Yes, this is she," Grace said, and then her face fell, like the dough she had been punching. She turned her back to Franny. In a voice that was not much more than a whisper, she said, "Where," and then, "Thank you for your trouble," and "That was very kind of you." She hung up and with maddening slowness turned around.

"Who was that?" said Franny.

"A woman who found your music book with my unmailed letter in it in the bathroom of the Margaret Sanger Clinic," Grace said.

"Oh," Franny said.

In one theatrical gliding movement, Grace got down on her knees before Franny and took Franny's hands in her sticky, floured hands, letting her glasses remain at the end of her nose. She stared myopically into Franny's face. "Franner Danner, is there anything you want to tell me?"

"No." Franny pulled back her hands. "I happened to be passing and needed to use the bathroom."

The look of heartfelt concern persisted, and then Gracie sighed. She rose to her feet. "Okay," she said softly. "Okay, but when you want to talk, honey, just know I'm here for you."

"Here for me?" Franny stood up and got out of the kitchen fast. She ran up to her room, slammed the door, and took out her journal.

"She knows I followed her now," she wrote feverishly. "She knows I'm onto them, so she's trying to throw me off the scent by pretending that it's my problem. I don't understand why Gracie does this. Has Hyacinth sworn her to secrecy? Why won't she confide in me? It would make everything easier for all of us. How do I convince her that I'm not too young to handle what she has to tell? How do I let her know that *nothing shocks me*. I am not the baby of this household."

She put down her pen and thought over what Grace had just said. She realized that Grace thought she, Franny, might have gone to the clinic for a problem of her own. This thought caused a

hot blush to flood her neck and cheeks. Franny
said out loud, "Grace thinks I'm the one who's in
trouble."

This was so absurd that if Franny hadn't been
so busy blushing, she would have laughed. She
shoved the idea out of her mind, picked up her
pen, and wrote:

HERE IS WHAT I MUST DO

1. I must let Wilson know that he can open
   himself to me and tell me about his pain.
2. I must let Mom know that marriages can
   survive rough patches, and if they don't
   and there is a divorce, we can survive.
3. Must let Dad know that men commonly
   suffer a M.L.C.* at his age and that sometimes a young woman represents lost youth,
   etc., etc.
4. Must let all of them know that they can
   talk to me and I will listen.
   * Mid-Life Crisis

She put down her pen. She hadn't felt so good
for ages. She was not only calm and happy, but
superior and adult. She sat down at her desk and
finished her math. Then she went two assignments
ahead in science and polished off her French.

All through dinner that night Grace made big
questioning eyes at her.

Mr. and Mrs. Dillman didn't seem to pick up on her looks.

"This is the most delicious chicken," Mr. Dillman exclaimed. "Honestly, Esther, I don't know how you do it. Children, this mother of yours is a marvel."

Testimonials to Mother? A clear admission of guilt. Franny wondered why she was the only one at the table who knew that.

Mrs. Dillman accepted the compliment with a smile.

At the first break in the conversation Grace focused her full attention on Franny. "Fran, when I saw you in the hall today at school, I wish you'd said hello."

"You looked busy."

"Never for you, sweetheart. We're sisters. You come first. Anytime you want to speak to me, please."

"Sure," Franny said hurriedly.

"What a nice thing to say," Mrs. Dillman said.

Franny thought they sounded like a TV family. Canned sighs and laughter should punctuate their dinner-table talk.

"It's just that I won't have that much time to be here with all of you," Gracie went on, speaking in a low tone. "Time goes so fast. Next year I'll be away at college and it will be over. I'll have hardly gotten to know you at all."

Franny couldn't believe her ears.

"I mean, our life is so busy and familiar, I just thought it would go on forever. But of course I know it won't, nothing does. . . ." She stopped speaking and picked up her water glass, all choked up.

"These are wonderful sentiments, dear," Mrs. Dillman said softly, "but your going away to school won't be as final as all that. You'll be home for vacations and intersessions and summers, no matter which college you choose."

"But it won't be . . . like this," Gracie said. "Franny is growing up so fast."

"I'll slow down," Franny said.

"I just wish I knew you better," Gracie said.

"If I weren't sitting here, I wouldn't believe this," Wilson said.

"Wilson," Mrs. Dillman warned.

"It's like being in the middle of one of Hyacinth's operas."

"I'll let that pass," Gracie said in her normal voice. She darted a nasty look in his direction. "One day you will consider yourself privileged to be anywhere near Hyacinth and her operas."

"Baloney," Wilson said. "She sounds like a chicken."

"I'd like to know what you know about chickens or the opera, for that matter."

"About as much as you do," Wilson said.

"Then you must know that last Saturday, Hyacinth sang for one of the leading coaches at the

City Opera and that he agreed to take her on. I was there. She was *fantastic*."

"Hyacinth did that?" Mr. Dillman said.

"We were not going to tell anyone until it was absolutely definite," Gracie said.

"Was she wearing her cape?" said Mr. Dillman mischievously.

"Oh, Daddy." Gracie was full of scorn. "She was superb. She'll have a great career."

"*Puck, puck, puck, puck, puck, puck.*" Wilson flapped his arms at his sides and did his brilliant chicken imitation.

"Wilson," Mrs. Dillman ordered, "stop."

Franny had to laugh, though she didn't want to. It was interesting to her to note the way Wilson tried to conceal his infatuation for Hyacinth by making her an object of fun.

"Whatever you may think of her," Grace said, "please remember that she is my friend, Wilson. I would hope you could show her some respect on my account."

Wilson stopped clucking. His arms fell to his sides and he looked terribly upset. "I'm sorry, Gracie," he said and swallowed so that his Adam's apple fell like a plumb line. "I think she's okay. It's just that she's singing all the time. It's so weird, you might say."

"*You* might say," said Grace. "You don't know her well and you have no appreciation of her extraordinary gifts."

"Yeah," Wilson said to his plate.

Franny caught the tragic undertone in his voice. She alone at the table was aware of Wilson's heart-breaking appreciation of Hyacinth's "gifts."

Franny excused herself. She ran upstairs to write all this down before she forgot a single nuance.

She handed in her Monday journal entry in place of a book report. Once again she took the caution to mark it CONFIDENTIAL, and she changed the names to initials.

"October 27. W is suffering mad jealousy over the filler of the cape. He knows his passion is point-less. He suspects H is pregnant, but does he know by whom? Can he contain his jealous passions? This is Shakespearean. I am sitting on a volcano at home. I can only cross my fingers and hope I'll be prepared when it erupts."

When she handed this entry to Mrs. Propper on Tuesday morning, it was with fingers cold as ice.

At lunch, Lisa Tetarsky sat down next to her. "Why are your journals marked confidential?" she said.

Now this was a significant development. Lisa was part of a group that Mrs. Dillman described as "fast and flashy," and that Franny described as "popular." The Lisa group was so clearly removed from Franny's circle that you could almost detect ropes around it. Aside from these invisible ropes, there were at least five other groups in descending popularity to separate sophisticated, fashionable

Lisa and Company from the likes of chubby Franny, weepy Rosy, and blabbermouth Mary Beth.

Lisa's group of girls came up to school on the same bus. Starting in the fourth grade they had been interested in who liked who and which boy paired up with which girl.

All this made Franny nervous. Mrs. Dillman disapproved of "growing up too fast." She would say, "You take your time, Franny. There are lots of years to be grown-up in. Don't let yourself get pushed into doing things you don't feel comfortable doing."

Easy enough for *her* to say. She didn't have to hear Lisa say, "Write up a list of all the boys who love you, and then make a list of all the boys you love." Or, "I'm making a party but nobody can come who doesn't have a date."

Gracie had laughed. "Date? Nobody even uses that word anymore."

Easy enough for *her* to laugh. There was no Lisa Tetarsky in her class. There was no Josie Dennis with her perfect little French jeans and twenty thin gold bangles and original Frye boots. There was no Muffy Dewey with her flirty eyes and soaring giggles and Italian (yes, Italian) schoolbag and eighteen-inch waist. Gracie's class had been simpler from the start and Gracie had been one of its shining lights.

"My journal is marked confidential because I

don't want anybody to get hurt," said Franny, not looking at Lisa.

"Really?" Lisa widened her almond-shaped eyes and lifted her plucked brows. "Is it dynamite?"

"Maybe," said Franny.

"But darling," Lisa drawled, "you're such a simple, homespun child."

"You never know. Still waters and all that."

"Mmmmm hmmmm. Betty got a peek and she says it's enormously hot stuff."

"Betty is disgusting."

"She can't help that," Lisa said. "But will you do a reading? All dressed up in a new pair of overalls?"

Franny was about to answer when she saw something so disturbing that Lisa Tetarsky and her questions were swept from her interest.

Through the window in the door of the lunchroom, Franny saw Mrs. Propper engaged in conversation with Grace. They both looked very serious. This was odd indeed. Grace didn't have Mrs. Propper for anything. They were in different divisions. There was no reason why Grace should be talking to Mrs. Propper. The only thing they had in common was herself, Franny Dillman. Something was going on. Something was up. It made her lose her appetite.

"Excuse me," Franny said. She moved so fast that she heard her milk carton topple. When she opened the door to the lunchroom, both Gracie and Mrs. Propper turned at once.

Gracie colored so quickly that the heat brought tears to her eyes. "Hi, Sib," she said. She had never called Franny that one before.

"Hello there." Mrs. Propper pressed the clipboard she was holding to her breast.

"We were just, I was just asking Mrs. Propper about stories for the yearbook," Gracie said. "We would love to have something in the yearbook to represent the middle school. Stories, poems, essays."

"That is such a nice idea," Mrs. Propper said. "There is a great deal of talent to tap. In fact, I've been thinking of starting a literary magazine just for the middle school." She looked at Franny. "Would you be interested in working on something like that, Fran?"

"Yes, I would," Franny said.

The bell rang. Grace said she had to run. Mrs. Propper waved good-bye, and as she did so, Franny noticed that the top paper on her clipboard was marked CONFIDENTIAL.

5

〰〰〰〰〰〰〰〰〰〰〰〰〰

"I can just guess what they were talking about," Franny wrote in her journal later that day. "They were discussing *me*. Propper was asking Gracie about our family. I wouldn't blame her for being a little curious at this point. What did Gracie make out of it? I'll have to wait to find out." Franny put down her pen and reread all her journal entries to date. She liked them. She was getting some good dramatic problems and scenes down on paper. She felt she had the stuff of a lively journal. But when she reread what she had written a second time she was disappointed. Something was missing. What was it? Oh yes—"hard to handle" material that Mrs. Shuloff would not let Rosy read. In all four of the books she had just read, the heroines referred to their developing bodies and the new sensations these bodies experienced. In *For Keeps* Pammy described her lovemaking in blow-by-blow detail. The heroines were like characters in a biology textbook. Then and there Franny decided to liven up her own journal with a good bunch of words describing the human reproductive system.

She knew her parents had a couple of interesting books high up on the living-room bookshelf. There were diagrams and charts in these books. They were called *Human Sexuality* and *So You're Going to Have a Baby*, and such. She closed her journal, went downstairs, climbed onto a stool kept near the shelves, and took down a few dust-covered volumes.

Half an hour later, when Gracie came in, Franny was deep in a complicated illustration of the fallopian tube. She thought *fallopian tube* was very straightforward as words went. Gracie came up behind her on her crepe soles and switched on a reading lamp.

"Hi, Franner Danner," she said in her new TV sitcom voice. But when her eye fell upon the open book on Franny's knee, she gasped. Her face filled with anguish. "Oh, Fran," she crooned. "Can I help you?"

"No." Franny pulled away slightly.

"Look Pumpkin, sweet Sib. I'm here for you. What do you want to know? I mean, you shouldn't have to worry about things and not share them. I'm here to share them with you. Do you know that, Franny?"

The telephone rang.

"Let it ring," Gracie said halfheartedly.

But it stopped ringing and then Wilson came in. "It's for you, Fran," he said. "Alan Nungazer."

"Alan Nungazer?" Gracie repeated, falling back on her heels as if the name were a charge of dynamite that had rocked her off balance. "Alan Nungazer," she said again. This time she made the name sound like the answer to a question.

Her reaction surprised Franny almost as much as the fact that Alan Nungazer had called her.

Alan said, "Hello," very stiffly. Then, in a rehearsed-speech way, he went on. "Mrs. Propper has asked me to call a handful of people to discuss plans for a middle school literary magazine. She suggested your name. She thought you might have something to contribute as well as your time. We'll need people to read and do paste-ups, et cetera, et cetera."

"How much time?"

"Every Wednesday afternoon, about an hour and a half. We'll have an open meeting tomorrow to get things started, elections, et cetera, et cetera."

"I suppose I'll be there," Franny said flatly, trying not to sound as pleased or excited as she was.

Alan told her where they would meet the following afternoon and said, "et cetera, et cetera" at least four more times before he hung up.

She went to the kitchen to celebrate being chosen as "one of the handful." She took out peanut butter, a jar of sour pickles, and a brownie. But

while she ate she felt strangely full. It was the opposite of her Fashion Box Booteek dressing room
sensation, the opposite of feeling as if a deep hole
were opening up at her feet or the feeling she had
when she saw her own reflection in the mirror. She
had been chosen to work on the middle school literary magazine. Mrs. Propper had suggested her.
Alan Nungazer had called her. She sighed deeply.
It was like stepping into a soft, warm room after
roaming around in a cold, dark hall. It was like ar-
riving at last at one's own place.

Grace came in. "I put those books away. I hope
you were finished with them."

"Mmmmmm." Franny's mouth was full. "I was
reading up about the cervix and the fallopian tube
and the womb." She said these words with relish,
hoping that Grace would be impressed. Hoping
Grace would realize that Frances Dillman was a
person to contend with.

"It's so very important that you satisfy your curiosity on those points," Grace said, swallowing hard.

"It's not just curiosity that motivates me," Franny
said after a moment. "It's related to *us*, Grace. My
interest is close to home. It's here."

"Tell me about it," Gracie pleaded. She pulled up
a chair.

"Not for *me* to tell." Franny screwed the cap back
on the jam.

"For whom, then?" Gracie importuned.

"If *you* don't know," Franny said rising, "I cannot tell you." She turned on her heel to put the

food away. Out of the corner of her eye she saw her sister tug her hair back from her face and heard her mutter, "What am I going to do?" like a character in "As the World Turns."

Before she went to bed, she wrote in her journal. "This is turning into a poker game between me and Grace. She thinks I have something to tell her. I *know* she has something to tell me. We are each waiting for the other to begin. She told us she's going to Lincoln Center with Hyacinth on Saturday. I think this is a way to get me *not* to follow them to the clinic. Wilson keeps staring at me. He's onto something new. He lifts weights and does push-ups. Also, he's growing sideburns. This family trouble had better resolve itself soon. I don't know how much longer I can stand it."

She closed her journal and turned off her light. She lay still, staring at the shadows that glided about on her ceiling. The house was quiet. She thought how, beneath that stillness, hearts and minds were enduring unimagined torments. She decided to wear her gray jumper to school the next day. She would wear it with a blue blouse. In honor of the middle school literary magazine she would not wear overalls. After she decided this, she fell asleep.

The next morning between classes Alan Nungazer approached her in the hall. Alan approaching resembled a lighthouse moving through small boats. He was very tall. His glasses caught the light like a flashing beacon. He had a habit of not bothering to look down at the person he was talking to so that whomever it was (in this case Franny) felt like a floundering vessel trying to make contact. Alan spent most of his spare time in the library. He had read Tolstoy when he was in the sixth grade and knocked off Thomas Hardy in the seventh. He was known to be brainy and weirdly brilliant. Franny had listened to Hyacinth and Grace "go on" about him for years.

"Guess what Alan's reading now?" was a common opening for Grace after a visit to Hyacinth's. At first Franny liked to believe that Alan had perpetrated a clever hoax. She was sure that he skimmed through the books in order to get a reputation, leaving them around the house in obvious places and holding them up in front of his face whenever he could. But she learned that this was not the case. Alan didn't boast about his reading. He didn't advertise it. He loved novels. It was that simple. At times he did refer to something he had read, but it was no more than what anybody else would have done.

"We'll meet at three-thirty, not three-fifteen, and in Miss Angstrom's fourth-floor room, not Miss Jeb's. If you have any ideas, write them down. Also, tell people about the meeting. It should be open. I've put up some notices on the bulletin board on the third floor." He inclined his head slightly so that his glasses winked at her. "Hyacinth tells me you've been writing up a storm."

"How would she know?" Franny said, as much to herself as to Alan.

"She's your sister's best friend, isn't she?" he said. "They're on the bloody telephone every other minute shrieking like a pair of banshees over something or other."

Franny grinned. "Yes," she said. "Sometimes I wonder if they're mental."

"That would be the best we could hope for." Alan sighed. "Then they could be medicated."

At that precise moment Franny decided that Alan Nungazer was a worthwhile human being. "Have you seen your sister's cape?" she said.

"Seen it? I've had three allergy attacks from it. Every time I come into a room I find her standing in front of the mirror doing the Mad Scene."

The bell rang.

"I'll see you later," Franny said.

As she walked to her next class she decided to fit Alan Nungazer into her plot. Who could he be? He was obviously not a hero type. He wasn't a villain either. At any rate, there were no villains in the books she had been reading. Then it came to her. He would suit very nicely as the confidant. The friend that every heroine needs to pour her heart out to.

At lunch Muffy Dewey and Lisa Tetarsky pulled up chairs at the end of her table. "I understand you and Alan are putting together some sort of literary magazine for the middle school," Muffy said.

"It's an open thing. We're having our first meeting this afternoon."

"I saw the notice." Muffy spread a selection of raw vegetable strips before her and began to munch on them like a delicate rabbit. "Has Alan read your confidential journal?"

"Nope."

"Will he? He loves literature."

"I don't know." Franny looked over at Rosy Shuloff for help. Rosy looked away.

"Whatever your tactic may be, I wish you luck with Alan. He is unconquerable," Muffy said, chomping daintily.

"In other words, she's got a thing about him," Lisa explained to Franny.

"Had it since second grade." Muffy sighed. "The doof has never even noticed. I'll certainly be at the meeting."

Franny stopped eating. Was this possible? A *thing* about Alan Nungazer? Since second grade? She looked at Muffy in disbelief. How could she be so different from those girls? Who was right? Who was normal? She bet that Muffy and Lisa loved to talk about their developing reproductive systems, just as her new heroines did. She could no more bring herself to discuss such things than to write about them. Were they using boys the way she had thought Alan used his reading? To attract attention? Or was she, Frances Helene Dillman, abnormal? Was the basis for her friendship with Rosy and Mary Beth the subjects they did *not* dis-

cuss, instead of the ones they did? She had never
had a *thing* about anybody her own age. Mr.
Rochester, Mr. Crawford, Mr. Fitzwilliam Darcy
in *Pride and Prejudice*, Mr. Traxell the pharmacist;
but Alan Nungazer? She lost her appetite.

She looked out over the tables of the lunchroom. She was very upset. Her eyes fell upon Mike
Hanratty. His teeth were bound in wire. His greasy
hair fell in solid sheets on either side of his face.
He didn't change his shirt from one month to the
next, and somebody had once caught sight of the
top of his underpants, gunmetal gray. Did anybody
have a *thing* about him? It was grotesque.

"Incidentally, I like the jumper," Lisa said. "It's
sweet."

Franny nodded. She watched Muffy fold up the
waxed paper that had wrapped her strips of carrot
and celery. Then she stared grimly at Muffy's tiny
waist, belted in purple suede. She got hungry again
and finished her potato chips.

Later, at the meeting, Alan was voted editor, and
he appointed three associates, one representative
from each grade of the middle school. Franny was
his appointee for the eighth grade. She was to take
submissions of stories, poems, essays, and drawings,
as well as help to select the work for the magazine.
They set up committees of readers and paste-up,
layout people. Alan ran the meeting in a cool, de-
tached, efficient way. There was no joking around
with Alan. Even when Muffy volunteered to do the
layout, she was businesslike.

"Did Grace tell Hyacinth about my writing?" Franny asked Alan when the meeting was over.

"I guess so," he said. "But they exaggerate and dramatize so that I throw away ninety percent of everything they say."

"What *did* they say?" Franny felt her heart stop cold.

"I don't remember, to tell you the truth." He closed the conversation so abruptly that there was no going on with it. Rosy Shuloff was standing right behind them thrumming on her loose-leaf.

"What was that about?" Rosy said as soon as they started downstairs. "All that writing stuff. Is it the confidential journal?"

"I don't know."

"Are you keeping a real, true journal, Fran?"

"What do you mean?"

"I mean some people keep journals that are just a lot of bull. They make stuff up and pretend to have feelings they don't really have."

"Which people are those?"

Rosy thought for a moment as she put on her mitten. "Everybody," she concluded. "I never read a journal or diary I trusted. Even the ones that were hidden. They all sound made up to me."

For some reason this did not offend Franny. In fact, she found it a relief. She was beginning to worry about just how honest she was in her own journal.

She and Rosy started the walk home. The day was raw. They kept their hands deep in their pockets and watched their breath form cloud puffs in front of their faces.

"D'you want to stop at Traxell's?" Rosy said.

"Sounds good to me," Franny agreed. She would have liked that idea at any time of the day or year. Traxell's was one of her favorite places. It was a drugstore with soda fountain. Everything about it —its smells, its sights, its sounds—brought her a sense of well-being. No matter what storms swirled about her in her life, at Traxell's she found comfort. She would order an egg cream, take a twirl on her stool for old times' sake, breathe in the odd mixed smell of cosmetics, soap, toast, fried grease, and burnt coffee, and feel better. But there was even more to Traxell's than these delights. There was Mr. Traxell himself. In Franny's opinion, Mr. Traxell was the older Mr. Rochester. Whereas Mr. Crawford resembled Mr. Rochester as Jane first knew him, Mr. Traxell was Rochester at the end of the book, after his bitter year of suffering. Like Mr. Rochester, Mr. Traxell had lost one eye. Furthermore, he had a proud aloof manner which caused her to become practically faint. He held himself superior to everyone who entered his shop, never made small talk, never did anything much but scowl and fill out prescriptions. Once, years ago, Muffy Dewey had spilled milk on a stack of fresh newspapers and she told everyone he nearly smacked her. Franny had been interested ever since.

As they crossed into the street a block away from Traxell's, Franny turned her head to the side to look at a window display in the bakeshop. She had a sense of a fleeting image behind her. It was her sister Grace, darting into a doorway.

"She's following me," Franny muttered under her breath.

"What?" Rosy said.

"My sister."

"Yeah," said Rosy. "She's been trailing us since we left school. Hyacinth too. I wondered when you'd notice. They've been creeping behind the parked cars and diving into doorways. Can you beat that?"

Franny stopped walking. "What are they doing now?" She bent down to pull up her knee sock.

Rosy half-turned her head. "They just darted into the doorway of Fein's Hardware. They're looking at a log splitter."

Franny started to walk again, then she broke into a run. "Race ya," she shouted to Rosy. They ran the rest of the way to Traxell's.

Mr. Traxell was not visible except for the top of his elegant head in the back of the high enclosure where he made up prescription drugs. Along the Formica counter top there were clear plastic domes beneath which Danish and crullers were stacked. By this time of day they were a bit soggy and shopworn, but Franny loved them that way. Added to an egg cream they made the best snack on earth.

She selected a coffee ring from the bottom of the heap. Rosy ordered a hamburger. She was anemic.

"Why is Grace following you?" Rosy asked as soon as they got their food. "What's up?"

"Lots of things," Franny said. "None of which am I at liberty to discuss with you."

"I can't believe this," Rosy said. "All of a sudden you've turned yourself into this incredibly mysterious character. I feel like I don't know you or something. I feel as if I'd just teamed up with the pages of a book or a movie. This is so strange. It's not like Daily Life." She was gesturing with the hands that held the hamburger, and already there were globs of ketchup on her chin. "In fact, I don't believe it. I think you've made it up and you've put these crazy ideas that are in your *head* into practice, and they're catching." She swallowed. "Like a cold. I've caught your crazy ideas. Like when you told me about Mr. Crawford being Mr. Rochester, I believed you." She shook her head. "Well, I'm not that dumb anymore. Let me assure you of that." With one greasy finger she pushed her hair behind her ear and stared loftily at her reflection in the smoked-glass mirror that ran the length of the counter.

"Suit yourself," Franny said, as indifferently as she could. "But I'd like to know what you make of what's going on in Traxell's window."

Without moving their heads they both swiveled their eyes around to see out the large plate-glass window that faced the street.

Peering through the glass were two slouched figures with their collars drawn up around their ears. Grace and Hyacinth.

"Oh, Franny," Rosy breathed.

That night Franny wrote in her journal. "Something is actively brewing. Aside from Grace and Hyacinth trailing me all over, they were on the phone with each other for seventy-five minutes. When I came into the room Grace smiled at me and stopped talking right in the middle of a sentence. There was no giggling at all. She looked as if she had been crying.

"Mom continues to be oblivious. She came home from work actually singing. That woman has worked out a set of defenses to rival the Great Wall. She doesn't let anything get to her. Not her wasted talents, not her husband's betrayal, not her eldest daughter's duplicity. Nothing. She just keeps trucking, making her *New York Times Menu* meals and marking her math papers. She pretends that her life is not about to fall apart. Maybe it's conceited of me to write this, but I'm glad that she has me, Frances Helene Dillman. I will help her to pick up the pieces when her house of cards collapses."

Franny copied this journal entry into her notebook using initials for names. She wrote CONFIDENTIAL across the top of the page. She had decided not to worry about turning journal entries in. She had gotten a lot of mileage out of them—Lisa and

Muffy's interest, Gracie's hysterical anxiety, not to mention Alan Nungazer's attention. Handing in her journal had turned out to be worth the risk. At least so far.

6

After Mrs. Propper's class the next morning, however, Franny changed her mind.

"Are your folks splitting up or something?" Josie Dennis asked her in a pointed whisper as they gathered their books for study hall.

Franny was shocked. "No, what are you talking about?"

"I couldn't help but see a little part of your journal. It was kind of on top of Mrs. Propper's clipboard. I hope you're not angry about my looking. I read the whole page, Fran. I just wanted you to know that I've gone through it. My folks split up two years ago." They had begun to walk together toward the study hall. "You described my early feelings so feelingly. Have you read *Life Goes On, I Suppose?*"

Franny nodded.

"Well, it's just like that, isn't it? Remember how awful Nellie feels while her parents are holding back all their tensions, and everything is kept under wraps, and she can't understand why they want to split? That's the stage you're in now. Wait till they start screaming. Believe me, it will get better." She thought for a moment. "It also gets worse."

"I can't wait," Franny said morosely.

"I felt so helpless during that time of tension," Josie recalled. "You described the situation so well, Fran, it was uncanny." She stopped walking to put a hand on Franny's arm. "If you need to talk about anything, please talk to me. It's hell going through these things alone. They *do* get better. Really." She laughed harshly. "Either that, or they get worse."

Later, Alan Nungazer stopped her outside the lunchroom. "What's going on at your house?" he said. "Hyacinth spent all afternoon mooning around the house. She didn't sing once. Said she'd been given some tragic news she couldn't talk about, and it had to do with *you.* My mother tried every trick she could think of to worm it out of her. What's up?"

"You wouldn't believe me if I told you," Franny said.

"Try me."

She gave him a long look which he actually returned. He had nice round gray eyes that were surprisingly trusting.

"Not here. Not now."

"Where?"

"I'll meet you at Traxell's. Four o'clock."

"Okay."

It would be good, she decided, to tell him about Hyacinth and her father. Somebody else had to know. Someone who could support Hyacinth in *her* hour of need. Also it would help Franny to share the burden of her knowledge. And she had already decided to cast Alan in the role of confidant to the heroine.

She got to Traxell's before Alan and so was able to flip through the magazines.

"Can we talk here?" he said over her shoulder.

"No." She adjusted her knapsack straps, mortified to have been found deep in an issue of *Screen Gems*. "We better take a walk."

They left Traxell's and crossed the street to a park where benches circled an empty sandbox and row of swings. The day had turned raw. Franny snapped the collar of her jacket closed and plunged her hands into her pockets. In a passing car window she saw her reflection. The down tiers of her jacket, stitched on the horizontal, made her look, she thought, like a row of hot dogs laid side to side on a grill.

"I'll put it straight, Alan," she said. "I'm reasonably sure that Hyacinth, your sister, is pregnant."

"Who?" Alan stopped walking and almost toppled to one of the empty benches. "Who?"

"Hyacinth." She sat down beside him on the edge of the bench.

"Hyacinth?"

"Hyacinth, your sister."

"Why?"

"Many clues, Alan. Think about it. For one, there is the cape."

"The cape?" He turned away from her and stared at the swings. "But she doesn't even go out with guys. Who could it be?"

"Oh, Alan." She could hardly breathe. She had no idea she would get this emotional. She dropped her head. "My father."

"Your father?"

"Or maybe some singing teacher at Lincoln Center. It's been so awful for me. Ever since I figured it out, Gracie's been harassing me and hounding me to tell her what I know. She knows I'm onto something. I think she helped Hyacinth, and Wilson is in love with Hyacinth, too. I'm almost sure of it. My mother doesn't suspect a thing."

Alan had pushed his face into his hands. His elbows were on his knees. All she could see was his hair. "This is ridiculous," he said. "You don't know anything at all except that my sister bought a terrible ratty old cape and goes around singing the 'Mad Song.'"

"I followed them last Saturday."

"Where?"

"To the Margaret Sanger Clinic, where I thought

they'd go for birth control and abortion information."

"Did they?" He still hadn't looked up.

"No," she admitted bitterly. "I miscalculated. They went to see this guy at Lincoln Center. But maybe they'll go to the clinic this Saturday."

"What makes you think so?" Alan finally picked up his face. He was looking at Franny as if she were a lunatic.

"Because I know from my instincts and from things I've read about their age group, the way they talk and think."

"You're going to follow them Saturday?"

"I'm going to go back to the clinic. I'm reasonably sure they'll be there." She hadn't actually planned to do this. She wanted to prove to Alan how strongly she trusted her intuition.

"I'll be there too," he said.

"You will?"

"I'll be there all right. This is crap, Frances Dillman." He stood up.

"Two-thirty," said Franny.

"Two-thirty," said Alan. She wrote the address of the clinic on a piece of paper torn out of her assignment pad. As they left the park, Franny saw the tip of a velvet cape disappear behind Traxell's window along with the heel of a familiar fur-trimmed boot.

As soon as she got home, Franny recorded her interview with Alan in her journal. She allowed

herself some florid descriptive passages on the subject of the "lowering lead-gray clouds" and the
"gloomy overhanging branches of the bare trees,"
which "echoed and reinforced the mood of tension" between herself and Alan.

Then she wrote, "I don't know exactly why
Grace and Hyacinth are following me. Does Grace
really think the unthinkable? That I am the one
who is in trouble, same as Hyacinth? Is this how
they delude and distract themselves? Or do they
suspect that I am onto them?"

There was a knock on her door. "It's me, Wilson.
Can I talk to you, Fran?"

This was a first. Not since the days when he
played railroad engineer and needed her to be
passenger; or boss of the office and needed her for
secretary; or space man and needed her for Mar-
tian. Had Wilson knocked on her door asking for
a Talk? The journal and her new life of journal
keeping and plot finding had worked a miracle.

"Come in," Franny said, setting her notebook
aside.

"Look, Fran," Wilson said, awkwardly stepping
into the room. "I don't know what's going on
around here. I thought maybe you could help me
out."

"What do you mean?"

"I mean, everything is so weird. Grace is wringing her hands and crying and I think it has something to do with you. I think," he lowered his voice
and sat on the edge of her bed, "I think that Grace

and Hyacinth have been tailing you. They're very worried about you, and that is a quote."

"Hah," Franny barked. "That's rich."

"Are you okay?" said Wilson.

"I'm okay," Franny said. "In fact, I may be the only one who is." She gave him such a penetrating look that he dropped his gaze. "Are you okay, Wilson?"

"Huh?" He pulled at his sideburns.

"Are you okay? You are a fourteen-year-old male and I worry about you. I worry about how you never express your innermost feelings. Is it part of some macho image you have of yourself to keep everything bottled up inside? Does it go with 'pumping iron' and putting me down? I worry about *you*, Wilson."

Wilson stood up abruptly. His face was flushed. "Okay, can it," he said angrily.

"Wilson," Franny said and rose, "I just wanted to help you."

"I certainly have no intention of receiving aid," he said. "I thought that there were strange vibrations in this house. It seemed to me that they centered around you. Look, Fran," he stopped right in the middle of his anger and appeared helpless. "I'm sorry if I hurt your feelings sometimes. I'm sorry if you're in any kind of trouble. That's all I wanted to say, basically. If you need anything, let me know." He left her room.

"Need anything from you?" Franny said to the closed door. She opened her journal and quickly wrote, "Wilson just left after a very strange scene. I have a feeling that he wanted to confide in me but he chickened out at the last minute. He tried to make the trouble look as if it was mine. This, incidentally, is Gracie's technique."

She closed her journal. It was five-thirty, time to go down and help Grace with dinner.

Neither Grace nor Franny mentioned having seen each other through Traxell's window. They worked together preparing dinner without speaking except for, "Did Mom say to set the oven at three-fifty?" "Yes, are you washing the greens? Where's the olive oil?" and "Did you see me grease the casserole, I forget."

Mrs. Dillman had left the dinner makings on the table, and a recipe was magnetized to the side of the refrigerator. She did this whenever she had a late day.

"Where is Mom, anyway?" Franny asked.

"A meeting at our school, sweet sibling. I think it has to do with the book fair."

"Is she running it again?"

"No, but she's got to pass the torch to Mrs. Krouse. She's run it since I was in the fourth grade." Grace was chopping an onion in precise cubes, so it was impossible to know what made her eyes so drippy.

"I wish you wouldn't call me that," Franny said.

"What?"

"Sib and sibling. It sounds so phony."

"I *am* sorry," Grace said icily.

Franny knew she had offended her but she went on. "I have a name," she said. "It's *my* name and it is not dependent upon my relationship to you."

Suddenly Gracie's anger dissolved into heartfelt compassion. "Oh, of course, of course you have a name. Oh, Franner Danner, I am so sorry. How could I have been so unfeeling. Especially *now*."

Between her teeth Franny said, "Don't call me Franner Danner."

"I won't call you anything," Gracie spat back.

They stared at one another from opposite sides of the kitchen table. Enough tension flowed between them to have lit a small fish tank; at least that was the way Franny decided to describe it in her journal.

The front door slammed shut, and Mrs. Dillman's piercing "hello" rang through the house, followed shortly by Mrs. Dillman. It was obvious she was agitated. So agitated that she had not bothered to hang up her coat or remove her hat.

"That was the most peculiar meeting I have ever attended at any school," she said, yanking off her left glove. "Is there any coffee left to reheat?" She glanced over at the stove. Grace poured some leftover coffee into a pot and set a light under it.

"What happened, Ma?"

"First of all, someone named Mrs. Dennis, a rabbity-looking bean pole of a woman, took my elbow and told me that when I am ready I should join a group called Single Again. She said they run clinics on Parenting, Money Planning, Alimony, and Joy. Then a lady called Mrs. Chris Dewey said that she had just joined Club Sahib Harachachacha and there were better men there than anyplace in town, including the Young Republicans. All the time I was trying to tell them how to organize the book fair, they kept making cow eyes at me. The whole thing gave me the creeps. I didn't even stay for coffee."

Grace filled a cup with hot coffee and pushed it in front of her mother, who had finally removed her coat.

"So help me, I've never met two more neurotic women," she said. "It's good to be home again."

Franny burst into tears and ran out of the room. Mrs. Dillman's baffled gaze followed her till there was nothing but the sound of Franny's crying in the upstairs bedroom.

◇◇◇◇◇◇◇◇◇◇◇◇◇◇◇◇◇◇◇◇◇

7

Friday dawned gray and overcast. There were
low-hanging clouds and an unpleasant, fitful wind
that howled from the north and rattled the window
above Franny's desk. She awoke with a nervous
jangling sense of not having slept very well. She
was worried about Saturday. She dressed for school
in her overalls, trying to pretend that everything
was normal. Down in the kitchen Grace stood at
the stove cooking oatmeal. Her eyes were down-
cast, her expression flagrantly tragic. Wilson was
wolfing down leftover spaghetti in the furtive way
that drove Franny wild. He had combed his hair
forward and slicked it down on his forehead so he
looked like Moe in the Three Stooges. Both Wilson
and Grace regarded Franny guiltily, as if they had
just been talking about her.

"Morning," she said.

They grunted. Wilson propped a book up in front of his face. *Microbe Hunters.* Grace spooned oatmeal into a bowl. "Would you like some, Fran?" she asked in a hospital hushed voice.

"No, thanks. I'm on a bagel kick. Bagels and ice cream with anchovies. Yum."

"We don't have anchovies," Grace said, alarmed.

"I was kidding."

"You were?" Searching look.

They sat eating together as if they were waiting for Skylab to fall. Upstairs Franny heard her father's shower running, and then the radio went on. Mrs. Dillman always listened to the news while she dressed. This morning all these familiar things seemed laden with new, distressing overtones. Franny couldn't wait to get out of the house.

But school was no different. She found it impossible to keep her mind on anything. She would focus on some ordinary problem too hard and then miss the explanation. She couldn't pay attention or understand.

"Boy, are you keyed up," Rosy said as they went into the lunchroom. "Is something new going on that you are 'not at liberty to discuss'?"

"I don't know," Franny said.

"Hey, can your brother really lift one hundred and fifty pounds?" Mary Beth piped in, out of the blue.

"How should I know?"

"You live in the same house."

"Sometimes it smells like Stillman's Gym," Franny said with disgust. "Un, un, un," she grunted, imitating Wilson lifting weights.

"Don't be like that," Mary Beth said reproachfully. "You ought to consider yourself lucky to have a brother like Wilson. He's so . . ." She paused and then dreamily whispered, "so all-around."

"All-around?" Franny sneered. "Like fallout, he's all-around."

They sat down at their usual table and began to unwrap their sandwiches. Franny always took a bag lunch from home and supplemented it with odds and ends from the school cafeteria.

"Can I join you?"

She looked up from her egg and baloney on seeded roll to see Alan Nungazer looming between Mary Beth and Rosy.

"Uh huh." The two girls parted like the Red Sea so that he could sit opposite Franny. Nothing of this sort had ever happened before.

"There are a few things I want to discuss with you re the lit mag," Alan said in his prim voice. He set his tray down carefully. "The cover, for one." He had bought the special hot lunch. It lay congealing in his plate. Franny couldn't take her eyes off it.

"The cover is very important," Alan said. "I don't know if we should change it for every issue or keep the same one. I want some feedback about this."

He poked his fork into the stuff on his plate that resembled corn. "You know, it's got to somehow say who we are."

"Uh huh," Franny nodded. "I see what you mean."

"I'm going for milk," Rosy said. "Want something, anyone?"

"I'll go with you," Mary Beth said. They left.

Alan leaned across the table toward Franny and in a lowered voice said, "I wanted to tell you, I'm reading Brontë."

"What?"

"I sort of heard through Hyacinth how much that book meant to you, and influenced you, and I wanted to tell you how impressed I am, much to my surprise, by Charlotte. Of course Emily is the genius, but Charlotte holds her own."

"Oh, stop," Franny cried, putting her hands to her ears.

"What?" Alan's glasses blinked.

"Just don't, don't talk to me about it like that. Brontë? Who is Brontë? Some, some writer? I don't care about some writer. And stop snickering about what you *heard* about me."

"I'm not snickering." He looked scared, in fact. He'd put his fork down and was tipping his chair back as if he thought she might attack him.

"Yes, you were too snickering! Grace told Hyacinth about me and Jane Eyre and Mr. Rochester and Mr. Crawford, and you were too snickering,

Alan Nungazer. I can tell a snicker from a stare."
Her voice had risen so that a few nearby heads
were turning.

"I was not snickering," he insisted. "I was simply
trying to commend your taste."

"*Commend my taste?* I don't need *you* to commend my taste." She got up from the table. "And
don't talk to me about Brontë again. I read *Jane
Eyre*, not Brontë."

As she stalked out of the lunchroom she noticed
that Muffy's admiring gaze followed her right to
the door.

That scene would have been enough for one
ordinary day, but there was more to come.

She went home immediately after school. Often
on Fridays, it was Mrs. Dillman's habit to buy
bread and cookies from an Italian bakeshop near
where she taught. These cookies were hard as rocks
and full of hazelnuts. Franny would make a cup of
hot cocoa and dip a cookie till it turned to a divine
mush.

There was no one at home. She went up to her
room, unloaded her book bag, and opened her
closet. She decided to calm herself by making spe-
cific preparations for Saturday. She would select
her clothes and set them out. After some consideration she chose her gray jumper. She hung it on her
closet door. Then she went downstairs to make her

cocoa. She was in the middle of stirring the milk and mashing out lumps of powder against the side of the pot when the doorbell sounded.

She turned off the heat under the cocoa. "Drat."

Larger than life, in her flowing cape stood Hyacinth on the landing. She had topped herself off with a broad-brimmed, green velour hat, into the band of which she had tucked a plume.

"Grace isn't home."

"I know." She glided into the foyer. "I've come to visit *you*, Francesca mia."

Franny's stomach cramped like a muscle. She wondered if it *was* a muscle. Wilson would know. "Me?"

"You." Peals of operatic laughter rang out. "You look surprised. Why should you be? I've known you and loved you for years. I feel now as I have always felt about you—simpatico. You are like my own little sister. Why should it be strange that I come to see *you?*"

"Because you're Gracie's friend."

"Does that mean I cannot be your friend?" Her eyes grew wide and sad at this thought. She took off her hat and threw it onto the hall table where it knocked down a candlestick. She ran her fingers through her unruly mane of dark hair. "Will you ask me in, Francesca mia?"

"Sure." Franny stood aside for her to pass. "I was just making cocoa. Want some?"

"Love some. Bella, bella." Rubbing her hands together she followed Franny into the kitchen where

she paced back and forth while the cocoa was
heated and poured into mugs. Franny set four of
the hard cookies in a bowl and brought it to the
table.

Hyacinth cleared her throat as she would were
she about to begin an aria. She removed her cape
carelessly, letting it slip to the floor. Then she set
both elbows on either side of her steaming mug.
Her large brown eyes beamed upon Franny. "This
is so *good*," she said. "This is so *right*. You and me
for a visit, a tête à tête."

"A tête à tête?" Franny dipped her cookie.

"At last. Yes, I will say it. At last. I have always
felt this simpatico feeling for you. We are alike.
Oh, Grace is my friend; sensible, stalwart, practical,
sane Grace. How I love her! But our temperaments
are poles apart. Whereas you, Franny, are my kind
of people. Passionate, volatile, emotional, quick to
love without restraint, an artist." As she said the
words "love without restraint," she lowered her
head over the mug and kept her eyes pinned to
Franny's. "Of course you know what I mean?"

"No."

"No? Ah, Francesca." She reached out one hand,
knocked down a salt shaker, and grabbed Franny's
finger off her mug. "Don't hide from me. Don't
close off from me. Don't, don't. We can help one
another. I will open myself to you. You must open
yourself to me."

Franny was confused. She couldn't figure out

what was happening. Did Hyacinth want to confide in her? Or was Hyacinth trying to wheedle information out of her by suggesting an exchange of some sort? Was she an agent for Gracie? "What do you want to know?" Franny said cagily.

"Let's talk about love." Hyacinth leaned back and sighed. "Let me tell you how it is for me." She lowered her voice. "I have a Mr. X, Franny. His hair is gray at the temples. He is mature. He is brilliant. He is sophisticated. Whatever he wishes of me, I have decided I will not hold back. Why? Because I am an artist. What I feel, I will use in my work. Already the Nungazer sound has deepened, matured, become fuller, richer, and more profound."

Franny sucked on her cookie. This was pretty good stuff. She decided she had been right. Hyacinth really was in trouble, just as she, Franny, had surmised.

Hyacinth stopped talking, took a sip of cocoa, and leaned toward Franny. "Now *I've* told you about *my* Mr. X. For me it is May and September. In your case it is April and April, yet I will understand. Share with me as I have shared with you, Francesca mia. You will feel better, as I feel better. That is why I am here. Talk to me, unburden yourself as you cannot to those in your family. I came to listen."

Franny stood up in panic. "I have nothing to tell. I don't know what you're talking about."

"Okay," said Hyacinth crisply. She picked up her cape and adjusted it. "If that's how you want it." She rose. "I suppose you're not ready. I hope it won't be too late when you are." She paraded out of the kitchen, took her hat, and let herself out the door.

Franny collapsed on a kitchen chair. That was where Wilson found her ten minutes later. "Save me some of those," he said of the cookies. It hadn't even occurred to her to eat them. He went up to his room, and soon she heard the comforting jingle of his barbells.

She tried to play the piano, but couldn't concentrate. None of the old magic worked. After three or four attempts with a Mozart minuet, she gave up. She started back to the kitchen. In the front hall her reflection came at her like an avenging fury. She decided to stand still and confront it head on. She looked hard and long. She had to admit that what she saw was interesting. The face was troubled. Its green eyes were clouded, its dark, thick brows drawn down. The white, smooth cheeks, if sucked in, revealed bones (hooray) that were positively captivating. The lips, when brought down at the corners, were cynical in a nice way. What a provocative face, Franny marveled. As she stood there before the hall mirror admiring herself she heard the kitchen phone being dialed. Then she heard Wilson's voice sounding raspy.

"Oh, hi, is Mary Beth there?" it said.

Franny looked at her pale face in the mirror. This could not be happening.

"Oh, hi, hi, hi. Hi there, M. B."

M. B.?

There was a moment of frightful goatlike bleating laughter. "Well, so how goes. Un huh. Uh huh. Yeah, right. Like yo ho. Yo right, uh huh. Okay right. Tomorrow sounds agood. So why don't I meetcha at Traxell's and we'll just amble us over to the Orpheum and take a look."

The movies. He was going to take Mary Beth to the movies.

"Right. See ya tomorrow, one o'clock." He hung up.

Franny heard him whistling. She swam back to the piano. He went up to his room. The barbells clanged from above . . . *un, uh, uh, uh.*

Mary Beth and Wilson? She leaned her head on the keys. Mary Beth Blabbermouth had not breathed a word of anything. Why did she, Franny, have to hear this now? Just when she needed support and encouragement to face her tomorrow? Why were all these strange, unforeseen events being thrust upon her? Events which had nothing whatsoever to do with Her Plot. Why?

She sat up. The answer came to her. She was being tested. All heroines were tested one way or another. This was her test. Tomorrow she would prove herself. She went upstairs to select the sweater she would wear with her gray jumper. As she fished in her drawer she comforted herself.

1. Hyacinth was still pregnant.
2. Hyacinth's lover was still an older man.
3. Grace was still hysterical.
4. Mrs. Dillman was tense.

Everything was okay.

8

Rosy took the news worse than Franny would have predicted. "You told me you wouldn't ditch me again," she complained. "You promised, and there were witnesses."

They were standing on the subway platform. It was Saturday morning, and a train was coming.

"Can't you understand, an emergency has arisen," Franny screamed against the noise of the oncoming train. "I promise you, I'll never do this again."

"I don't believe your promises," Rosy said bitterly. "Why didn't you call me and tell me before so I could make other plans?"

"I didn't think you'd have them."

Rosy drew herself up with dignity. "A lot you know."

They got into the train and sat down. Franny remembered Mary Beth and Wilson. Did Rosy have a developing secret life too? That would be unbearable. "I'm at a crossroads," she said. "Everything is terrible. I don't expect you to understand, but please don't judge me." She wondered where she had read that.

Fortunately, Rosy wasn't wondering the same thing. She appeared to soften. "Okay, Fran," she said. "But don't do this again. Swear."

"I swear."

The entire morning at music school gave Franny a feeling of déjà vu. Once again she was ditching Rosy, once again she was going to prolong a lunch by herself, and once again she was setting out to test her theories. Theories based on a book she believed in to such a degree that she couldn't remember sometimes where *it* left off and her own life began. The difference between this Saturday and last Saturday, she recalled with a pang, was that she would not be alone. Alan Nungazer would be there testing her and challenging her. It was one thing for Mary Beth Higgens to tease her by announcing that Mr. Crawford was a "joker"; it was quite another and more serious thing for Alan Nungazer to topple her entire scheme of suppositions with a cold "I thought so. You are a lunatic" stare. After yesterday, she suspected he would be bent on vengeance.

As she headed downtown she felt panic rising. She wondered if she could be so wrong. She was too tense even to eat the beefburger, cole slaw, and french fries she ordered. The only way she was able to get them down was by taking small sips of egg cream between mouthfuls. The luncheonette where she ate had none of the soothing qualities of Traxell's. The waitresses screamed at each other and flung silver and china around so there was a constant din. By the time she paid her check she was worn out.

Alan was waiting for her on the corner in front of the church where one week before she had stood in the rain. It was not raining today. A sharp wind blew from the east. Alan had his hands deep in his pockets. He looked like part of the church's arrangement of odd funnels. He was scowling at the doorway to the clinic building. When he saw Franny, his expression hardly changed. "This is the craziest idea," he said. "You were nuts to have thought it up, and I'm even more nuts to have agreed to meet you." He was angry with her, all right. The scene in the lunchroom had done it. She was filled with regret.

"How long have you been waiting?"

He looked at his digital watch. "Precisely seven and three-quarters minutes. I'll give you precisely seven and three-quarters more."

"Seven minutes? But they may be late. Hyacinth is always late."

"And you expect me to stand here waiting into eternity for some figment of your imagination to materialize. I'm cold. I'm going in."

"It isn't seven minutes, you can't."

"Why not? We can just as easily wait in the lobby and get out of this wind." He started for the building with Franny walking unwillingly at his side.

"Oh, please, Alan," she said. "If we hop up and down and change corners we'll stay warm. Please."

"People will start throwing quarters at us, and God knows what fantasies that will trigger in your brain."

They had just reached the entrance to the clinic's building, when, looking up at the same moment, they saw Hyacinth and Grace approaching them from the corner.

"Looook," Franny breathed out in a long sigh. She felt enveloped by warmth and safety. Righteousness swelled within her to such a degree that she felt taller. She had been tested and she had been *right*.

Grace ran up to them. Her face was drawn into such serious lines that she looked years older, like Aunt Alice Terkel who lived in Troy. "So you've both come," she intoned in a dramatic, low voice. "I wondered if you would. I'm proud of you, Alan. I'm proud of you too, Frannery Dannery. Very proud."

Franny was confused to the point where she didn't know what to say.

"Actually I don't know what you're talking about," Alan said. "We are taking a walk."

Hyacinth leaned over and kissed him on the

cheek, managing to knock off his glasses. "Little brother," she sang, "what a good man you are."

"We're going to the UN," Alan said quickly. He was the color of baked brick. "Just happened to turn down this street. Coincidence of Dickensian magnitude."

"And we're going to the Whitney," Grace said in her most artificial Englishy voice. "Just happened to turn down this street too."

"Coincidence, coincidence," Hyacinth chimed, like an operatic chorus.

"We'll be seeing you." Alan grabbed at Franny's arm and pulled her west. Gracie and Hyacinth stood for a moment waving good-bye and then headed east.

None of them noticed that not one of them had gone into the building.

After walking at a very fast pace for over a block, Franny said, "What do you think now, Alan Nungazer?"

"I think it's very complicated," Alan said.

Franny felt cheated. She had expected an apology. She wanted him to admit that she was right. "That isn't what I meant," she said.

"I know, you want me to° say you were right and I was wrong and you're not crazy. I won't though, because we really don't have much to go on."

"We don't?"

"Not enough. However, I will grant you, you won that round."

They went down into the subway, which was not much warmer than the street, but at least there was no wind. Waiting for the train, Franny said, "Some people read a lot, Alan, but they don't involve themselves in the books. They kept themselves aloof. They hold themselves away from the action. They read to judge and to analyze. Some of us read with passion. We let ourselves go, and we learn something about life."

"I don't know about that." Alan shook his head. "I think some people read books to forget who they are. They don't know where to draw the line. It's not uncommon, especially if the reader's own life lacks excitement and drama. It's known as escape." He looked down at her. His round gray eyes were so bland and actually timid that Franny could hardly believe he had said something that reverberated through her to the depths of her being.

She was enraged. "Some people," she yelled, for the train was coming, "are dead from the neck up. They talk that way, they read that way, and they live that way. I feel very, very sorry for them. They are missing out."

Alan looked at her skeptically. He drew his lips together and lowered his head. "I don't know about *that*," he said. "And I doubt that you feel sorry for them."

On the subway he took a book out of his pocket, and except for looking up occasionally to see what stop they were at, he read *The Forsyte Saga*. Franny read the ads.

It wasn't till Franny got home that she was able to celebrate her victory. Of course this celebration was conducted in the kitchen. As soon as her coat was hung up she made for that nice place. She heaped up a plate of leftovers from the refrigerator. There was a chicken leg, rice, and half a head of lettuce. She daubed the chicken with a generous dollop of ketchup and filled a glass with root beer. She put a spoonful of vanilla ice cream in the root beer. She arranged all this on a tray to take up to her room. When she got to the front hall she was accosted by her reflection in the mirror. This caused her to go back to the kitchen and return the half head of lettuce. The next time she passed through the front hall she remembered to avert her eyes from the mirror and made it safely up to her room. She set the tray on her desk and took out her journal. She would indulge in the luxury of writing about her triumph while eating.

She was so engrossed that she was only dimly aware of the slam of the front door and her mother's "halloo." Later on she heard Grace come in and call, "Mother, are you home?" and her mother's answer. Then she heard murmuring voices on the landing and footsteps downstairs. She smelled something delicious; bread baking and onions cooking in butter. She had finished her cold chicken and rice and her journal entry for the day. She was rereading parts of *For Keeps* when there was a knock on her door.

"Fran, are you busy?" Mrs. Dillman said.

"No, come in."

"Darling," Mrs. Dillman stood nervously on the threshold. "Can we have a little talk?"

"Sure, Mom."

Mrs. Dillman perched at the edge of the bed. She looked flushed and her eyes were troubled. "Listen, sweets, Gracie just told me a few things that concern me."

"What things?" Franny's heart raced. Here it was. The denouement. It was about to begin. She was ready. Nothing shocked her. She would be needed. At last they would come to her.

"About your music book being found at the Margaret Sanger Clinic. About her having gone to find out what was up, and meeting you with Alan Nungazer in front of the clinic this afternoon."

So that was how Grace planned to play it. She was not going to tell the truth at all. She was going to make Franny do the dirty work. Make Franny be the one to explain. Franny decided she would not do that. She wouldn't help Grace cover up. Grace would have to do her own explaining. "I just went in to use their bathroom," Franny said, looking away from her mother's face.

"But darling, what were you doing in that part of town?"

"Taking a walk."

"In the rain? We're talking about last Saturday. What drew you to that area?"

"Family matters."

"I don't understand." She bit her lip till it turned white.

"Certain things are going on here, Mom, things that involve all of us and that may give pain, but that really need to be seen in a clear light."

"Please tell me."

"It's not for me to do that." Franny looked down at her journal. "All I can do is give some sort of comfort when the time comes. Let you all know I understand."

Mrs. Dillman's mouth fell open. "I don't understand, dear. The time for what?"

Franny sighed. "The time when we need one another. You probably think I'm just a child and don't understand. But, Mom, I've read a great deal, and I have deep sympathies, and when the time comes, I'll be ready."

"Can you give me some clue about when the time will come?" Mrs. Dillman asked in a whisper.

"Isn't it usually nine months," said Franny, "give or take a few?"

"Oh, my God," said Mrs. Dillman as she lurched from the room either to throw up or pass out, Franny wasn't quite sure which.

❖❖❖❖❖❖❖❖❖❖❖❖❖❖❖❖❖❖❖❖

9

Ten minutes later, Mr. Dillman appeared at
Franny's door with Grace and Mrs. Dillman.

"Dear Franny," Mr. Dillman said, his face looking like a very faded, run-down piece of used
furniture. "It might be a good idea if we all sat
down like the loving, caring family we are, and
worked this out so that we can make the kinds of
decisions that are best for you."

"For me?" She bolted to an upright position. "I
don't understand."

"Honey, Gracie has told us about the clinic. She
went down there to get whatever information she
could. But of course it's all very confidential."

"Don't be angry," Gracie implored. "We weren't
spying on you or judging you. We just wanted to
help."

"We never realized that Alan Nungazer meant anything to you," Mrs. Dillman said. "But I think it was so manly of him to have gone with you today." Her eyes filled with tears. "Really, I'm proud of you kids." Mrs. Dillman began to sob.

"Proud of us?" Franny repeated this, and fell back upon her bed. They had all three come into her room and formed a circle around her.

"You know, Esther, dear, if Fran doesn't mind, I think it might be an idea to call the Nungazers and ask them to join us on this. The problem does involve both our children. They are good people. What do you say, Fran? It's up to you."

"It's okay with me," Franny said, somewhat baffled. She wondered if her father meant to make a clean breast of everything in front of everybody and expose Hyacinth. She simply didn't understand any of what was happening. She had never intended that everybody confront everybody else. She thought she'd make private observations and then people would come to her individually and tell her all about themselves. These new developments had her in a state of confusion.

When Mrs. Dillman phoned the Nungazers she learned that they were expecting dinner guests. "Can't whatever it is wait?" Mrs. Nungazer wanted to know. When Mrs. Dillman said it couldn't, Mrs. Nungazer suggested the Dillmans come over to their house.

In the early dusk of that windy evening, Franny and Grace and their parents were fairly blown down half their street to the Nungazers' large stucco house, to share "that which concerns us both."

Mrs. Nungazer opened the door to her immaculate foyer. Mr. Nungazer towered behind her. Mrs. Nungazer's face was flushed. Her small, stout figure was overwhelmed by a flowered, lace-trimmed apron. Delicious cooking odors filled the room. Through the glass-paneled door to the dining room they could see the table already set with crystal and silver. Mr. Nungazer took their coats.

The Dillmans and the Nungazers had been neighbors for many years. Once a year the Nungazers had the Dillmans to dinner and the Dillmans had the Nungazers back. Mr. Nungazer was an accountant. He waved his hands around and talked a lot, like Hyacinth. Mrs. Nungazer taught piano. She was solemn and quiet, like Alan. Mr. and Mrs. Nungazer were opera buffs. Mr. Nungazer liked to boast that he did the books for two Metropolitan Opera tenors and a coloratura from the City Opera. He always said that these artists were hopeless when it came to managing their private affairs. Franny wondered how he would react when he learned how Hyacinth had been managing *her* private affairs.

"Hello there, Howard, Esther," Mr. Nungazer said in his high, chatty voice. "Sorry about this previous plan for dinner. We could have shared a turkey, family style. Grace, Franny, good to see you girls. My, my, my," he shook his bald head from side to side, ogling Franny. "Look how they grow. Only a minute ago, that one," he pointed to Franny, just in case nobody knew who he was talking about, "that one was sucking lollipops in her carriage." The thought of it started him chuckling. "I'll never forget it, Esther. You said you'd weaned her from the bottle onto lollies. She'd got them stuck all over the sides of her carriage. I never saw such a sticky little kid."

Franny decided that Mr. Nungazer was a creep. The Dillmans smiled thinly at his recollection.

"One day she'll accuse you of making her a sugar addict," Mrs. Nungazer warned sourly. "All they do is accuse us when they grow up."

"And if she hasn't any teeth left, she'll sue you," Mr. Nungazer went on happily. "Well, come on into the living room."

He ushered them in and with some hesitation added, "Please sit down." His hesitation was justified. The cushions of the sofa and chairs looked as if somebody had spent the afternoon inflating them with helium. Only a miracle of gravity kept them from floating up to the ceiling.

"Yes," Mrs. Nungazer sighed as if there were nothing else for it. "Do sit down."

They eased onto the sofa. *Pfffffft.* Mr. Dillman looked around. "Where is Alan? I think he should join us."

Hyacinth rose, extended one arm toward the staircase, and called, "Alan," with a vibrato it had taken her the last year to perfect.

Alan loped down the steps.

"Good evening, Alan," Mr. Dillman said softly. His eyes fastened upon Alan's face with tenderness and sorrow. "Good evening, my boy," his voice cracked.

"Hello." Alan looked around uneasily and remained standing.

Both Nungazer parents sat a little straighter, as if they had just been put on their guard. Then in his wobbly voice Mr. Dillman continued. "In the old days we would have beaten our breasts and said 'the children are in trouble,' but fortunately we live in different times. Our purpose should be to help, to support and comfort and guide, so that wise decisions can be made for Alan and Franny."

"Alan and Franny?" said Alan and Franny together.

"Why us?" Franny stood up. "I'm not in trouble. Alan's not in trouble. We just wanted to help."

"Help whom?" said Mr. Dillman.

"Hyacinth," said Franny.

"Hyacinth?"

"Why me?" said Hyacinth with a silly smile on her face.

"Because she thinks you're pregnant," said Alan in a bored tone.

"Is what?" said Hyacinth.

"Pregnant," said Alan. "Franny thinks you're pregnant."

"Me?"

"She thinks you wear that cape to cover up and

go to the Margaret Sanger Clinic for birth control
and she went to check you out. She dragged me
along to prove her point."

"*We* went to check *her* out," Gracie exclaimed.
"She left her music books there. Then we saw her
trysting with Alan near Traxell's and put two and
two together."

"I am not pregnant," Hyacinth stormed. "I am
simply Junoesque."

Mr. Nungazer was making a weird noise. It
turned out he was laughing. He had a high, strange
laugh. He fell back on the cushions and laughed
till he was gasping.

Mrs. Nungazer looked at her husband reproachfully. She was not a humorous person. "I would
like to know who you supposed the father of my
daughter's baby to be, Frances?" she said.

Franny thought her face would burn off. She
had never believed such an event as this could
occur.

"She thought the mystery man was Mr. Dillman," Alan droned.

"Mr. Dillman?" said Mr. Dillman.

"Mr. Dillman? Oh, Frances," said Mrs. Dillman.
Then she gave Franny a long hard look. Her eyes
narrowed to slits. "Frances," she said slowly, "what
have you been reading?"

"Those books you gave me," Franny replied.
"*For Keeps* and *Life Goes On, I Suppose*, and
Lord, Can I Call You Collect? and *It's Okay to
Cry a Lot.*"

"Oh, nooooo," Alan wailed, and sat down. "No wonder."

"No wonder what?" said Mrs. Dillman.

"She's been making her life into the plots of those books."

"I never bothered to read them," said Mrs. Dillman with regret.

"Wait a minute," Gracie said. "Have you been writing all this stuff into a journal for Mrs. Propper?"

"Yes," said Franny.

"Then that's why she stopped me to ask how things were at home."

"Did anyone else read those journals?" said Mrs. Dillman.

"A few people."

"Well, no wonder those women thought I'd need the Club Harachachacha." Then she started to laugh. Mr. Nungazer, who had caught his breath, began again, and then all four parents were laughing, even Mrs. Nungazer. They weren't just laughing. They looked zany and disgusting, Franny thought. They were falling back on the cushions and holding their chests and slapping each other's backs. Gracie began to laugh; Hyacinth joined in, trillingly. Franny gazed into space. Alan was staring at the rug.

"Oh, oh, oh," Mrs. Nungazer snorted. "If I didn't have these people coming tonight, I'd say we should all go out and celebrate."

Mrs. Dillman dried her eyes. "But wait a minute," she said. "The trouble all began with *Jane Eyre*. I'm responsible for switching Fran to those other books. What on earth should she read now?"

Alan stood up. *"The Rise and Fall of the Third Reich,"* he said like a shot, and left the room.

10

The Dillmans ended up having drinks with the Nungazers. Hyacinth burst into the "Bell Song" from *Lakmé*. Franny excused herself and went home alone with instructions to put a low flame under the casserole.

When she got to her own room, she sank miserably onto her bed. She felt shamed and humiliated as well as confused. She couldn't understand what had happened. She picked up her journal and read back through the pages. Then she picked up *For Keeps*. She opened it, but after a moment she threw it halfway across the room into the wastepaper basket. She knew she had been betrayed. She was angry as well as miserable. She remembered with a shudder the hilarious laughter at the Nungazers' and, turning over on her bed, pressed her face into the pillow until it hurt.

"Something is burning," Wilson called through her door.

"Oh, it's the casserole," she murmured. "I must have made the flame too high."

A few minutes later he said, "I turned it off, Fran."

"Thanks."

"You okay?"

"Nope."

"Oh."

She could hear him fidgeting and breathing outside her door.

"Do you want to talk to me?" he said.

"No."

She heard him shuffle back to his room. She realized that Wilson wanted to be nice. That he was really interested in helping her. She got even gloomier. The front door banged shut. Somebody put a record on, Vivaldi or Scarlatti. Pots were clanging in the kitchen. She heard the telephone ring. She felt utterly lost. Her entire world had collapsed. She was not only abandoned, but mortified. She could still hear Mr. Nungazer's high, awful laughter. At the recollection of it she raised both palms to her eyes to press hard enough to erase the picture of the laughing parents. It was the picture of her disgrace. They had all laughed. All except Alan, and he had been disgusted. She could not rid her closed eyes of that picture. Wet, sloppy, awful tears gushed out of their corners no matter how hard she might press. She wished she could go to sleep and wake up another person. She got part of her wish. She fell asleep.

When she woke up, she was still Frances Helene Dillman, and her mother was sitting on the edge of her bed. In the half-light, Mrs. Dillman was thumbing through the copy of *For Keeps* that she must have retrieved from the trash. She was smiling. When she saw Franny watching her, she leaned over and kissed her cheek.

"Dinner time, sweetheart," she said. "You had a nice nap." She got up, walked across the room, and carefully placed the book back in the wastepaper basket. "Why don't you wash your face and comb your hair and come downstairs."

That night and all the next day, her parents treated Franny as if she were recovering from an illness. It was right that they did so, for she felt that a very important part of herself had been cruelly removed. She suffered its loss as if it had been physical. Not an arm or a leg, but a lovely and necessary part of her mind had been amputated. Her family patted her shoulder and hugged her and spoke to her softly and encouragingly. But it was Monday she dreaded.

Monday meant Mrs. Propper and Alan Nungazer and Lisa and Muffy and Josie and Mary Beth (oh, no) and Rosy. The thought of it made her insides heave. She had to face them with nothing to fall back on, nothing to help her. She felt hollow and fragile, like a ghost. Gone was her world, gone the exciting landscape of her book-made dreams. "Over, buried, dead, wrong." She repeated those words to herself. She had been abandoned by books. She couldn't trust them, and she couldn't trust herself to read them. Without them life would be hopelessly dull.

On the way to school, Rosy said, "Stop moping, Fran."

"I feel like moping. *You* mope."

"Sure I do, but I depend on you not to. You've always got so much to go on about, you know."

"No, I don't know."

"The plots, the spying, even the poor grackle. I rely on you, Fran. You make life so interesting. Oh, Fran," Rosy said in exasperation. "You're exciting. Please don't be like this."

"I feel like it. Anyway, being the other way got me into big trouble."

"It did? Oh, tell me."

"Forget it."

They walked in glum silence the rest of the way.

She asked Mrs. Propper if she could see her for a minute after class.

"Those journal entries I handed in," she began with her eyes fixed on the desk blotter.

"Oh, yes, they're very interesting."

"Well, as it turns out they aren't entirely accurate. I meant them to be, but they aren't."

"No, matter, Fran." Mrs. Propper smiled. "They have a fine sense of the dramatic in them, and a very nice tension."

"But they aren't really true, as it turns out."

"Thank heavens," Mrs. Propper said. "What a relief."

Franny was suddenly relieved herself. "See, I was reading these books. I thought I was like the girls in the books and so I saw things in ways that weren't really the way they were."

"It can happen," said Mrs. Propper.

"Yes." Franny nodded.

"I once fell in love with the janitor of my building. I thought he was Heathcliff." Mrs. Propper winked.

"You did?"

In the lunchroom Alan asked her if she had gotten any good material for the magazine.

"A few things have come in. But I didn't get to read them yet."

"Yeah," he grinned. "You've been busy."

She didn't say anything.

"Would you like to go to this poetry reading at the Y?" he said.

"Alone?"

"No, stupid, with me."

"Oh," she said.

"I think you have an interesting mind," he said. Too shy to meet her gaze, he was looking at someone on the other side of the room. "I found some-

thing I thought was pertinent to your situation."
He took a book from his briefcase. Franny noticed
that his glasses were dirty. A napkin was stuck
between the pages of the book. "Read the part I
marked," he said, and turned to go back to the
lunch line.

She took the book. *Jane Eyre.* She leaned against
a wall near the door to the lunchroom and opened
to where the napkin had been stuck. She read.

> "It is vain to say human beings ought to
> be satisfied with tranquility: they must have
> action; and they will make it if they cannot
> find it."

She closed the book and looked around for Alan.
She saw the back of his head leaning over the
dessert display counter. He had understood something. Alan Nungazer may not be Mr. Rochester,
she thought, but he was a friend. Her spirits rose
like one of Hyacinth's better high notes.

That evening after the dinner dishes had been
cleared and placed in the machine and the pots
and pans were drying in the drain, Franny found
herself once again at loose ends. It was that time,
that special time, when it had been her habit to
go up to her room and write in her journal. She
glared at the table and chewed on her fingernail.

"Why are you glowering?" Gracie said.

"I have to write something for Mrs. Propper. I

don't know what to write. Everything in my life is dull and banal."

Mrs. Dillman folded up her towel. "I know what you can write," she said.

"So do I," Gracie nodded.

Franny sat down at her desk. She turned on the light so a sharp circle of it fell upon the clean, white, lined sheets of paper. She looked out the window and began to smile as scenes flickered before her eyes. Hyacinth twirling in her cape, Grace and Hyacinth darting behind parked cars, Grace wringing her hands, Frances herself lurking beside a concrete planter in the rain, Alan saying "I'll give you seven minutes," Rosy pleading for information. Her smile grew wide. She picked up her pen and, with the first feeling of peace she had known in days, she wrote . . .

"My mother thinks it all began with *Jane Eyre. . . .*"

Meet Glenwood High's fabulous four, the

SENIORS

Kit, Elaine, Alex, and Lori are very best friends. On the brink of graduation and adulthood, these popular seniors are discovering themselves, planning for the future, and falling in love. **Eileen Goudge $2.25 each**

- ____ #1 TOO MUCH, TOO SOON 98974-4-13
- ____ #2 SMART ENOUGH TO KNOW . 98168-9-19
- ____ #3 WINNER ALL THE WAY 99480-2-18
- ____ #4 AFRAID TO LOVE 90092-1-17
- ____ #5 BEFORE IT'S TOO LATE .. 90542-7-21
- ____ #6 TOO HOT TO HANDLE 98812-8-27
- ____ #7 HANDS OFF, HE'S MINE ... 93359-3-27
- ____ #8 FORBIDDEN KISSES 92674-2-19
- ____ #9 A TOUCH OF GINGER 98816-0-15
- ____ #10 PRESENTING SUPERHUNK 97172-1-23
- ____ #11 BAD GIRL 90467-6-22
- ____ #12 DON'T SAY GOODBYE 92108-2-31
- ____ #13 KISS AND MAKE UP 94514-3-19

TWILIGHT™

WHERE DARKNESS BEGINS...

☐	1	**DEADLY SLEEP,** D. Cowan	91961-4-47	$2.50
☐	2	**THE POWER,** B. Haynes	97164-0-49	2.25
☐	3	**THE INITIATION,** R. Brunn	94047-8-23	2.50
☐	4	**FATAL ATTRACTION,** I. Howe	92496-0-31	1.95
☐	5	**BLINK OF THE MIND,** D.B. Francis	90496-X-35	2.25
☐	6	**VOICES IN THE DARK,** J. Haynes	99317-2-25	2.50
☐	7	**PLAY TO LIVE,** C. Veley	96950-6-56	1.95
☐	8	**BLOOD RED ROSES,** S. Armstrong	90314-9-19	1.95
☐	9	**DEMON TREE,** C. Daniel	92097-3-18	1.95
☐	10	**THE AVENGING SPIRIT,** E. Stevenson	90001-8-58	1.95
☐	11	**NIGHTMARE LAKE,** C. Laymon	95945-4-15	1.95
☐	12	**THE TWISTED ROOM,** J.P. Smith	98690-7-16	1.95
☐	13	**VICIOUS CIRCLE,** I. Howe	99318-0-24	2.50
☐	14	**FOOTPRINTS OF THE DEAD,** J. Callahan	92531-2-20	1.95
☐	15	**SPIRITS AND SPELLS,** B. Coville	98151-4-	2.50
☐	16	**DRAWING THE DEAD,** N. Selden	92141-4-22	1.95
☐	17	**STORM CHILD,** S. Netter	98289-8-21	1.95
☐	18	**WATERY GRAVE,** J. Trainor	99419-5-30	1.95
☐	19	**DANCE OF DEATH,** L. Kassem	91659-3-10	2.25
☐	20	**FAMILY CRYPT,** J. Trainor	92461-8-32	2.25
☐	21	**EVIL ON THE BAYOU,** R.T. Cusick	92431-6-39	2.25
☐	22	**THE HAUNTED DOLLHOUSE,** S. Blake	93643-8-15	2.25
☐	23	**THE WARNING,** A. Byron	99335-0-15	2.25
☐	24	**AMULET OF DOOM,** B. Coville	90119-7-32	2.50

At your local bookstore or use this handy coupon for ordering:

DELL READERS SERVICE—DEPT. R706B
P.O. BOX 1000, PINE BROOK, N.J. 07058

Please send me the above title(s). I am enclosing $_____ (please add 75c per copy to cover postage and handling). Send check or money order—no cash or COD's. Please allow 3-4 weeks for shipment.

Ms./Mrs./Mr._____

Address_____

City/State_____ Zip _____

Judy Blume

Judy Blume <u>knows</u> about growing up. She has a knack for going right to the heart of even the most secret problems and feelings. You'll always find a friend in her books—like these from Laurel-Leaf!

___	ARE YOU THERE, GOD? IT'S ME, MARGARET......	90419-6-62	$2.50
___	BLUBBER.............................	90707-1-48	2.95
___	DEENIE.................................	93259-9-69	2.50
___	IT'S NOT THE END OF THE WORLD........	94140-7-37	2.75
___	STARRING SALLY J. FREEDMAN AS HERSELF......................	98239-1-63	2.95
___	THEN AGAIN, MAYBE I WON'T.................................	98659-1-15	2.50
___	TIGER EYES........................	98469-6-31	2.95

══LAUREL-LEAF BOOKS══

At your local bookstore or use this handy coupon for ordering:

DELL READERS SERVICE—DEPT. R706C
P.O. BOX 1000, PINE BROOK, N.J. 07058

Please send me the above title(s). I am enclosing $_____ (please add 75¢ per copy to cover postage and handling). Send check or money order—no cash or CODs. Please allow 3-4 weeks for shipment. <u>CANADIAN ORDERS: please submit in U.S. dollars.</u>

Ms./Mrs./Mr._____

Address_____

City/State_____ Zip_____

PAULA DANZIGER